ALFRED HITCHCOCK'S

Supernatural Tales

OF TERROR AND SUSPENSE

Here I am back again with as spooky a collection of ghosts and other supernatural things as ever kept anybody awake at night.

You will discover astonishing things about the long dead, the recent dead, and the undead.

If you are bold enough to read these eleven stories all the way through, I'll wager that you will see some familiar things in quite a new light.

Happy reading! Or should I say happy shuddering?

—*Alfred Hitchcock*

Alfred Hitchcock Story Collections
for Young Readers

Alfred Hitchcock's Haunted Houseful

Alfred Hitchcock's Ghostly Gallery

Alfred Hitchcock's Solve-Them-Yourself Mysteries

Alfred Hitchcock's Monster Museum

Alfred Hitchcock's Sinister Spies

Alfred Hitchcock's Spellbinders in Suspense

Alfred Hitchcock's Daring Detectives

Alfred Hitchcock's Supernatural Tales of Terror
and Suspense

Alfred Hitchcock's Witch's Brew

ALFRED HITCHCOCK'S

Supernatural Tales

OF TERROR AND SUSPENSE

Random House New York

The editor wishes to thank the following for permission to reprint:

Arkham House Publishers, Inc., for "The Triumph of Death" and "Mr. Ash's Studio" by H. Russell Wakefield, from the book *Strayers from Sheol*. Copyright © 1961 by H. R. Wakefield.

T. V. Olsen for "The Strange Valley" by T. V. Olsen. Copyright © 1968 by T. V. Olsen. Permission granted by the author and his agents, Lenninger Literary Agency, Inc., 104 East 40th Street, New York, NY 10016.

The London Mystery Magazine for "The Christmas Spirit" by Dorothy B. Bennett, "Slip Stream" by Sheila Hodgson, and "The Pram" by A. W. Bennett.

Helga Greene and Estate of Raymond Chandler for "The Bronze Door" by Raymond Chandler. Copyright 1939 by Street & Smith Publications.

Patricia Highsmith for "The Quest for 'Blank Claveringi' " by Patricia Highsmith, which originally appeared in slightly altered form in *The Saturday Evening Post* as "The Snails" in 1967, before being included in the author's story collection *Eleven*. Copyright © 1967 by Patricia Highsmith.

Harold Ober Associates Incorporated for "Miss Pinkerton's Apocalypse" by Muriel Spark. Copyright © 1958 by Muriel Spark.

Fedor Nikanov for "The Reunion After Three Hundred Years" by Alexis Tolstoy, from the book *Vampires: Stories of the Supernatural* by Alexis Tolstoy, translated by Fedor Nikanov. Copyright © 1969 by Hawthorn Books, Inc.

David McKay Company, Inc., and Jonathan Clowes for "The Attic Express" by Alex Hamilton, from the book *Beam of Malice*. Copyright © 1967 by Alex Hamilton. Published by David McKay Co., Inc.

The editor gratefully acknowledges the invaluable assistance of Henri Veit in the preparation of this volume.

First paperback edition published in 1983.

Library of Congress Cataloging in Publication Data

The Library of Congress Cataloged the First Printing of This Title As Follows:
Hitchcock, Alfred Joseph, 1899–   comp. Alfred Hitchcock's Supernatural tales of terror and suspense. New York, Random House [1973]. CONTENTS: Wakefield, H.R. The triumph of death.—Olsen, T.V. The strange valley.—Bennett, D.B. The Christmas spirit.—Chandler, R. The bronze door.—Hodgson, S. Slip stream.—Highsmith, P. The quest for "Blank Claveringi."—Spark, M. Miss Pinkerton's apocalypse.—Tolstoy, A. The reunion after three hundred years.—Hamilton, A. The attic express.—Bennett, A.W. The pram.—Wakefield, H.R. Mr. Ash's studio. 1. Horror tales. [1. Supernatural—Fiction. 2. Short stories. 3. Horror stories] I. Shore, Robert, illus. II. Title: Supernatural tales of terror and suspense. PZ5.H64Ap [Fic] 73-3694 MARC ISBN: 0–394-85622–8 (pbk.)

Manufactured in the United States of America   5   6   7   8   9   0

Contents

Attention, Suspense Fans!

Here I am back again with as spooky a collection of ghosts and other supernatural things as ever kept anybody awake at night.

In these stories you will discover astonishing things about the long dead, the recent dead, and the undead.

You will read about a country house where *some* people see horrifying sights and hear terrifying sounds . . . a vampire bat wing with an evil odor and strange powers . . . some sinister adventures aboard a model train.

You will encounter a doorway with something exceedingly peculiar on the other side . . . a flying saucer of remarkable design . . . an uneasy grave where the wishes of the deceased have been ignored.

If you are bold enough to read these eleven stories all the way through, I'll wager that you will see some familiar things in quite a new light.

Happy reading! Or should I say happy shuddering?

Alfred Hitchcock

ALFRED HITCHCOCK'S

Supernatural
—— Tales ——
OF TERROR AND SUSPENSE

The Triumph of Death

H. Russell Wakefield

"Amelia," said Miss Prunella Pendleham, "I have received a most impertinent letter this morning."

"Yes, Miss Pendleham?"

"It is from some Society, and it has the insolence to suggest that this house is haunted by ghosts. Now you know that to be false, utterly false."

"Yes, Miss Pendleham," said Amelia listlessly.

"Do I detect a hesitant note in your tone? You mean what you say, I trust?"

"Oh, yes, Miss Pendleham."

"Very well. Now this Society actually wished to send down an investigator to examine and report on the house. I have replied that if any such person enters the grounds, he will be prosecuted for trespass. Here is my letter. Take it and post it at once."

"Very well, Miss Pendleham."

"You always seem so glad to get out of the house, Amelia! I wonder why. Now make haste there and back."

A little later Miss Amelia Lornon was hurrying down the drive of Carthwaite Place. But as soon as she knew she was out of eyeshot from its upper windows, she slackened her pace. This she did for two reasons; she was feeling terribly frail and ill that morning, and to be out of that house, even for half an hour, meant a most blessed relief from that anguish which is great fear.

To reach the post office of the little hamlet she had to pass the Rectory. Mrs. Redvale, the Rector's wife, was glancing out of the drawing-room window at the time.

"There's Amelia," she said to her husband. "I've never seen her looking so ill. Poor creature! It's time you did something about her, Claud, in my opinion."

She was a handsome and determined-looking woman, and her voice was sharply authoritative.

"What can I do, my dear?" replied the Rector with the plaintive testiness of the conscience-moved weakling.

"You can and must do *something*. You can listen to me for one thing. I've been meaning to have this out with you for some time, ever since I realized what was going on. That sight of her convinces me it must be now, at once. If she dies without our having done a hand's turn to save her, I shall never know a minute's peace again; and I don't think you will either. Come quickly! Here she is going back."

The Rector reluctantly went to the window. What he saw brought a look of genuine distress to his kindly, diffident face. "Yes," he sighed, "I can see what you mean only too well."

"Now sit down," ordered his spouse. "I know we're in a difficult position; Miss Pendleham puts two pounds in the plate every Sunday, which is an enormous help to us. 'There are my servants' wages,' she seems to say, as she does it. But she is a very evil old woman; how evil, I don't think either of us fully realizes."

"Yet she *does* come to church," protested the Rector.

"Yes, she comes to church," replied his wife sardonically, "and like a great many other people for a quite ulterior motive; she wants to keep *us quiet*, and she bribes us to do so—don't argue—I know I'm right! Now we've been here only six months, but we've learned quite a lot in that time. We've learned that the Pendleham family have always shown a vicious, inherited streak; drunkards, ruthless womanizers, and worse, even criminals—and just occasionally a brilliant exception. This old woman is the last of the line, and it'll be a very good thing when the horrid brood is extinct, in my opinion."

"Of course," said the Rector, "we have to trust Miles's opinion for all this, *really*. And we know he's utterly biased against her; he won't even speak to her."

"He's been Churchwarden here for forty years, so he ought to know," replied Mrs. Redvale. "Besides, he loses financially by his attitude—she never buys a thing at his shop. He strikes me as a perfectly honest and sincere old man. Don't you think so?"

"I must say I do."

"Well then, what's his story? That she was crossed in love when very young, some other woman, as she believes, stealing her man away. So she made up her mind to have revenge on her sex in her own stealthy, devilish way. He thinks her mind was permanently tainted at that time; that she is actually, if not technically, insane."

"It all sounds so melodramatic!" murmured the Rector.

"Melodramatic doesn't mean impossible," answered his wife sharply; "there's plenty of *real* melodrama in the world. Now Miles says she has had five companions since she marooned herself in that house thirty-five years ago. Three have died there and two escaped quickly, declaring Miss Pendleham was a devil and the house hell. And now there's the sixth, Amelia; and she's dying, too."

"Dying of what?" asked the Rector.

"Of terror, if nothing else!"

"She could leave like those other two."

"That's so easy to say! You might say it of a rabbit in a stoat's snare. When you're sufficiently frightened you can neither run nor struggle. And she's in a hopelessly weak position; ageing, penniless, naturally will-less and pliant. She'd never summon up courage to escape on her own."

"But she seems, in a way, to like Miss Pendleham's company!"

"Simply because she dreads being alone in that *foul* house. Now you know it's haunted, Claud."

"My dear Clara, you put me in a most difficult position, because, as you know, I agreed with Miss Pendleham, there were no such entities as ghosts."

"Don't be a humbug, Claud! You said that only out of politeness and a desire to please. You knew it was a lie when you said it."

"My dear!"

"No cant! You remember, when we first went there, what was looking out of the window on the first floor?"

"There seemed to be something for a moment."

"Was it a small boy with his face covered with blood?"

"I got such a fleeting glimpse, my dear."

"Was it Miss Pendleham or Amelia?"

"No, I suppose not."

"They are the only people living in the house. And I told you what I saw when I went to powder my nose. I can see it now! Do you believe me?"

"I've never known you to tell a *pointless* lie. Yet a bush sometimes closely resembles a bear."

"But a little dead girl doesn't resemble a bush! And you heard that scream?"

"I thought I heard something—a curious cry—it might have been a bird."

"A bird! How would you like to live in that house with that sort of thing! You'd even—like Amelia—prefer Miss Pendleham's company to *Theirs*. It often makes me feel physically sick to think of her there. If we don't do something to save that poor woman,

I shall be plagued by remorse till I die!"

"Do me the justice, Clara, to believe that is becoming true of me, also."

"I wonder if you realize it as I do! I'm sensitive to places like that, and always have been. The very motes in the sunbeams there seem to make beastly patterns. I don't wonder Amelia is dying by inches, has been dying for years. She told me that when *They* are around her, the kettle will not boil. In other words, her brain is going as her body gives up the struggle!"

"Well, what can I do?" exclaimed the Rector. "Tell me, Clara! You are wiser than I in the affairs of this world, if I know more about the next."

"And if there is such a place!" rapped Clara.

The Rector sighed. "I'm deeply grieved you're such a skeptic, Clara."

"Nonsense! Every parson should have an agnostic wife; it keeps his mind alive. Well, we'll both think it over today and discuss it again tomorrow morning. I *mean* tomorrow. My mind is made up. As for that two pounds a week, could you go on taking it if Amelia died? Tomorrow at ten o'clock!"

"You were a long time, Amelia," said Miss Pendleham.

"I was as quick as I could be, Miss Pendleham, but my heart was palpitating so."

"Nonsense! You're perfectly well. Don't imagine things, Amelia!"

Miss Pendleham was one of those apparently timeless spinsters, so leisurely does the process of decay take its way with them. She was very tall and cylindrical in shape, an almost epicene, sexless body. She was invariably dressed in an iridescent gray garment of antique cut and rustling train. About her face, her nose in particular, the Rector had made one of his rare jests, by adapting to it a Max Beerbohm pleasantry, "Hints of the Iron Duke at most angles"; and, indeed, that ungainly, craggy feature dominated the rest. Her mouth was small, thin-lipped, dry. Her eyes were quite round—monkey's eyes—and an odd brimstone yellow, a family stigma. Her hair was a dense gray mass. The face was a mask, as though modeled in wax from a corpse, quite colorless. Her age might have been anything from fifty-five to seventy.

Amelia was about forty-eight. Once upon a time she might have been a bonny girl, for her features were well enough, but it required a sympathetic and perceptive eye so to scan and reconstruct the past. There are parasites which slowly devour and drain their hosts from within, till nothing is left but a thin, transparent envelope. A puff of wind and it disintegrates. Amelia might have been long entertaining some such greedy guest. Pounds underweight, gaunt and stooping, listless and lifeless of hair and eye, like a prisoner at long last delivered from a dungeon where she had lain neglected and forgotten. Death had his hand on her shoulder and was fast tightening his grip, but to give her her due it had taken nine hard years to bring her to this pass.

"I'll go and cook the luncheon," she said.

"Yes; what is there?"

"Chops."

"I'll have three. Are you hungry?"

"No, Miss Pendleham."

"Then cook four, and let mine be red right through."

Carthwaite Place rose on the northern slopes above Lake Windermere. It was unmistakably Elizabethan: a huge somber pile of brick with a multitude of mullioned, transomed windows and a flat roof. It had thirty-five bedrooms and one bathroom. It required many thousands spent on it to make it habitable, but that money would never be found; and it was very slowly breaking up and passing. The grounds surrounding it had gone back to a wild, disorderly nature. Miss Pendleham never left it, save to attend Matins on Sunday morning. Its one trace of modernity was a telephone, used for ordering her frugal wants from the market town six miles away.

Amelia dragged herself to the great stone vaulted kitchen and raked up the fire. She had begun to tremble again, and neve did she glance behind her. Once she paused as though listening, her face revealing the greatest anxiety. Several times her mouth moved as though she were muttering something, but no sound came.

Presently she finished cooking and took the results to the dining room where Miss Pendleham was already seated. The meal was eaten in dead silence and very quickly, for Miss Pendleham always attacked her food like a starving panther. On the wall facing Amelia was a tattered seventeenth-century tapestry. It depicted a company of knights and ladies riding in pairs along a sinister serpentine path. On the left of the path were three rotting corpses in open coffins. The air above them was thronged with vile flying things. Amelia's eyes always flickered around the room trying not to see it.

Miss Pendleham watched her covertly. At the end of the meal she said what she always said, "Wash up quickly and come and read to me."

"Very good, Miss Pendleham."

When she got back to the drawing room, Miss Pendleham handed her a book. It was a translation of the Abbe Boissard's life of Gilles de Rais, realistically illustrated. Amelia had already read it out endless times before. She read well, though the details of that abattoir ritual came oddly from her precise and virginal voice.

Presently Miss Pendleham stopped her. "Something very similar," she said in her high, metallic tone, "is known to have been done here by an ancestor of my own. He killed by torture a number of children, chiefly young girls, and employed their bodies for some such curious ceremonies. It is owing to that, possibly, that the house has acquired its quite *false* repute of being a haunted place. Perhaps I have told you that before?"

"Yes, Miss Pendleham," replied Amelia mechanically.

"I'm going to doze now. Wake me at five with the tea. Sit here till it is time to prepare it."

This was an ordeal Amelia detested, but had long accepted as part of her daily calvary. Was Miss Pendleham asleep, or was she slyly watching her? Were her eyes quite closed?

It was a soaking afternoon, the small dense mountain rain streaming down the windows. There was just that steady rain purr and the slow beat of the grandfather's clock to break the silence. Miss Pendleham never stirred nor did her breathing change. Slowly the light faded, and Amelia began to ache with stiffness and immobility.

Suddenly there came from somewhere in the house a thin high cry of pain. Amelia's eyes went wild and she put her hand to her throat. Miss Pendleham opened her eyes wide and slowly leaned forward, staring at her. "What's the matter, Amelia?" she said slowly.

"Nothing, Miss Pendleham," gulped Amelia. "I'll go and get the tea."

Miss Pendleham glanced after her bowed back. For a moment the mask was raised and she smiled. But the smile merely contorted the lower part of her face; her yellow eyes took no share in it. There came again that remote, agonizing wail. The half-smile vanished, the yellow eyes flickered, the mask came down again.

After tea she played Patience, and Amelia was left to her own devices till it was time to cook the supper. Anyone watching Miss Pendleham playing Patience, which is a stark test of virtue, would have decided that if he ever did business with her, he'd have kept a sharp lawyer at his elbow, for she always cheated when necessary, but never more than necessary.

Anyone who had watched Amelia presently preparing the supper by the light of two candles would have gleaned some understanding of the phrase "mental torture." Those candles threw strange shadows on the bare walls and arched roof. That observer might have caught himself imitating Amelia, glancing up fearfully and furtively at those crowding, multiformed shades, and learned her trick of flinching when she did so. Was that a small body lying prone and a tall figure with its hands to the small one's throat? And did that figure move? Just the flicker of the candle, of course. And yet that observer might well have wished himself away, but would he have had the heart to leave Amelia down there alone?

Supper was again a quite silent meal. Miss Pendleham scraped her well-piled plates tiger-clean. Amelia left half her sparse portions.

After supper Miss Pendleham said, "Fetch my wrap from my bedroom, Amelia; I forgot to bring it down." She said that almost every evening, perhaps because she knew how Amelia dreaded going up those dark stairs, ever since she had that fright four years ago.

Amelia fetched it, washed up, and returned again to the drawing room. "Now," said Miss Pendleham, "you can read to me for an hour. Get those stories by James."

* * * * *

"Well, Claud," said Clara next morning, "have you been thinking it over?"

"Yes, my dear, but I can't see my way clear, I'm afraid. We say she tortures these women. But *how* does she torture them? She gives them board and lodging, pays them something, I suppose—a pittance, no doubt, but something. She is superficially kind to them. She does not—could not—legally compel them to stay. Who would call that torture, save ourselves?"

"And Mr. Miles!"

"And Mr. Miles, if you like. Suppose I did tackle her. If she didn't at once show me the door, she'd probably call in Amelia and ask her if she had anything to complain about. 'No, Miss Pendleham,' she'd certainly reply; and what sort of fool should I look!"

Mrs. Redvale, like most women in the grip of logic, raised her voice. "You've got to be firm, Claud, and not be fooled by that sort of thing. You must take the offensive. She can neither sack you nor eat you. Tell her straight that you are certain Amelia is dying and must have immediate attention. Remind her three of her companions have already died in the house, and, if there's a fourth, some very awkward questions are bound to be asked. There *is* Amelia again! I'll get her in."

She hurried from the room and out into the street.

"How are you, Miss Lornon?" she said kindly.

"All right, thank you, Mrs. Redvale."

"You don't look it! Come in a moment."

"Oh, I can't! Miss Pendleham told me to hurry back with the stamps."

"Never mind; it's only for a minute."

Amelia hesitated and then reluctantly followed her in.

The Rector scanned her closely as he greeted her. Mrs. Redvale now assumed her most forcible manner.

"Miss Lornon, you're in a very bad state, aren't you? Don't be afraid to tell me; it will go no further."

Amelia began to cry in the most passive, hopeless way. "I suppose so," she murmured.

"That house is killing you, isn't it?"

"Oh, I can stand it, Mrs. Redvale."

"No, you can't! Have a good cry. You've *got* to get away from it!"

"I can't! Miss Pendleham would never let me go."

"She'll have to! Look here, Amelia—I'm going to call you that—we're determined to help you. In the meantime, remember nothing there can hurt you. They can frighten, they can't *hurt*."

"They can!" she sobbed. "They keep me awake nearly all night. In the summer it's not so bad, because they go away at dawn, but in the long nights it's terrible. I must go now."

"You won't have to stand it much longer! Bear up until we can do something."

"There's nothing to be done, thank you kindly, Mrs. Redvale. Oh, I mustn't say any more. Miss Pendleham would be so cross if she knew I was talking like this!"

"Nonsense! Your health comes before everything!"

But Amelia had hurried from the room.

"You see!" exclaimed Clara. "I could strangle that she-devil with my bare hands!"

"There's one thing I've never been sure about," said the Rector. "Does Miss Pendleham realize there's something the matter with the house? If not, the force of the charge against her is greatly weakened."

"Of course she does!"

"How can you be so sure?"

"I watched her when we heard that ghastly cry. She heard it, too, her demeanor showed it. But it doesn't worry her, she welcomes it as an instrument of that torture. She makes Amelia think, 'I must be going mad if I see and hear things that aren't there.' Can't you see what I mean? Her mind is diseased like that of her foul forebears. Those things are echoes of evil and she is utterly evil too. Did the 'first murderer' frighten the other two? Of course not!"

"Clara, that is a fearful thing to say!"

"You've just seen that wretched woman, haven't you! Look here, Claud, if you don't do something about it I'll lose all respect for you! This is the test of your Christianity and courage. *I'm* an infidel, but I'd do it myself if I thought she'd take any notice of me, but she wouldn't for she hates and despises all women. But you are her spiritual adviser."

"There's no need to be sarcastic, my dear."

"There's need to be something to goad you to action! Will you, Claud?"

"Oh, I suppose so," sighed the Rector, "but I wish I could consult the Bishop first."

"You'd get nothing but vague boomings. Is your courage at the sticking point?"

"Yes, I'll do it."

"Then go straight to the phone!"

He left the room and returned after a few moments. "She will see me at half-past nine tonight," he said.

"Did you tell her what you wanted to see her about?"

"I just said something of importance."

"And you were understating—it's a matter of life and death, and we both know it!"

"Have you been crying, Amelia?"

"Oh, no, Miss Pendleham, the cold wind caught my eyes."

"It doesn't seem cold to me. Give me the book of stamps and get luncheon ready."

During the meal Miss Pendleham said, "You see that tapestry, Amelia?"

"Yes, Miss Pendleham."

"You're not looking at it!"

Amelia glanced flinchingly up. She noticed that as each cavalier and his paramour reached the three open coffins, their smiles and lascivious glances changed to looks of loathing and horror. Because, she thought, they are young and happy and haven't learned to long for rest.

"It's called *The Triumph of Death*," said Miss Pendleham.

"Yes, so you've told me."

"That reminds me of something. Have you finished?"

"Yes, Miss Pendleham."

Miss Pendleham led the way into the drawing room. "Today," she said, "is the anniversary of the death of Miss Davis. She was my companion before you came. She was a foolish, fanciful girl in some ways. Have I told you about her before?"

"Only a little, Miss Pendleham."

"Yes, she was fanciful. She used to fancy she heard and saw strange things in the house and that shows her mind was tainted, does it not?"

"Yes, Miss Pendleham."

"I mean, if the house were haunted, we should both of us see and hear strange things, should we not?"

"Yes, Miss Pendleham."

"Which we never do?"

"No, Miss Pendleham."

"Of course not. Well, I should, perhaps, have dismissed Miss Davis earlier but I did not like to. Have I told you how she died?"

"No, Miss Pendleham."

"I thought not. I had noticed she was getting thinner, and stranger in her manner, and she told me her sleep was disordered. I should have been warned when she came running to my room one day saying she had seen a child butchered in the kitchen—and she had other hallucinations which revealed her mind was in an abnormal state. One evening I sent her up to fetch my wrap, just as I sometimes send you, and, as she did not reappear, I went in search of her. I found her lying dead in the powder closet of my room. The doctor said she had died of a heart attack and asked me if she could have had a fright of some kind. I said not to my knowledge. I think she must have supposed she had seen something displeasing. Look behind you, Amelia!"

Amelia started from her chair with a cry.

"What is the matter with you!" said Miss Pendleham severely. "I merely wanted to draw your attention to the fact that the antimacassar was slipping from your chair. I hope *your* nerves are not giving way. Didn't you imagine you had a fright of some kind a month ago?"

"It was nothing, Miss Pendleham."

"You screamed loudly enough. Bear Miss Davis in mind. Becoming *fanciful* is often the first symptom of brain disease, so the doctor told me; *hearing* things, *seeing* things when there is nothing to see or hear. Now you can read to me."

And this Amelia did, Miss Pendleham presently telling her to stop and *seeming* to doze off, while the windows rattled disconcertingly. As the light faded and the fire shook out its last flame and sank to its death glow, something white seemed to dart across the Musicians' Gallery and something follow it as though in pursuit, and there came that thin wail of pain. Amelia went rigid with terror.

"What's the matter, Amelia?" said Miss Pendleham, leaning forward in her chair.

"Nothing, Miss Pendleham. I'll make up the fire and then get tea."

While she was cooking the dinner that night she was thinking over what Miss Pendleham had said about Miss Davis. She had died of what was killing her, of course. She would die soon, now, very soon. She knew it, and then Miss Pendleham would get someone else, and one day that someone would die, too, for the same reason—unless—

Suddenly she paused in her work. What was that! Someone was crying in the servants' hall! That was something she'd never heard before. Her heart hammered in her throat, stopped horribly long, then raced away again. A piercing pain ran through her. Who was that crying? She must be brave. It might be someone *real* and not one of Them! She took a candle and tiptoed along the passage of the hall, a bare, desolate place reeking of dirt and vermin, which Amelia dreaded and seldom entered. There was no one there, but the sound of sobbing was louder. "Oh, God," moaned a voice, "I cannot bear it! I cannot bear it!" Then came a laugh, a sly sinister chuckle, and the wailing voice rose to a scream. "Oh, God, I cannot bear it!"

As Amelia went back to the kitchen her face twitched violently and uncontrollably. Was that *real* or not? Was it just a sound in her head as Miss Pendleham said it must be; just a *fancy*? If so, she was going mad like Miss Davis. What happened to mad people in that Other World? Were they mad *there*, too, and forever? That didn't bear thinking about. She must die before that happened. She *was* dying; she knew that by the terrible pains in her heart. What would happen when she was dead? Miss Davis had died; she'd just heard her crying. No, that was just a sound in her head.

Her face contorted again in the fearful effort to concentrate, to get it *straight* and clear in her mind. Well, she would die, like Miss Davis, and then Miss Pendleham would get someone else to look after her and it would all happen again with the new girl. No, it mustn't. It would not be right. Miss Pendleham was very kind, but she didn't understand about the house. It was all very curious and difficult, but it must not happen again. There was Miss Davis still crying, still crying in her head. But it would happen again unless—unless she was brave. If Miss Pendleham realized what sort of things happened to Miss Davis and her and what they saw and heard, she wouldn't let it happen, of course, but she didn't and so—

Did she hate Miss Pendleham? Of course not; why should she? Again St. Vitus racked her face. But it wouldn't happen again. There was the man and the little girl! She flung up her hands to her ears. A red veil was drawn down before her eyes. She shook her hands from the wrist and stretched and curved her fingers. The expression on her face became at once hard and vacant, like that of a beast at bay.

She retained that curious inhuman expression, and Miss Pendleham noticed it when she brought up the meal. It disturbed her and her own eyes went weasel-hard. Presently she said, "Eat your dinner, Amelia; what's the matter with you?"

"Nothing, Miss Pendleham. I'm not very hungry."

"Eat your food! By the way, you haven't been talking to the Rector or his wife, have you?"

"I just said good morning to Mrs. Redvale."

"Are you sure that was all?"

"Yes, Miss Pendleham."

And then there was silence for a time till Miss Pendleham rose and remarked, "You can read to me for a while," and Amelia read out a tale about some bedclothes forming into a figure and frightening an old man in the other bed.

"What did you think of that, Amelia?" asked Miss Pendleham.

"Very nice, Miss Pendleham."

"Nice! I don't believe you are paying attention. You read very badly again!"

"I'm sorry, Miss Pendleham. The old man was mad, wasn't he, Miss Pendleham? Like Miss Davis and *me*?"

Miss Pendleham stared at her. "Get my wrap!" she said brutally.

Amelia got up slowly and went through the door leading to the stairs. As she started to climb them she crossed herself and stretched and curved her fingers. A fearful twitch convulsed her face.

Miss Pendleham went to the front door, opened it and left it ajar and went back to the drawing room. Then, as the minutes passed, she cocked her head as though listening. There came that high torture-wail, and she straightened her head abruptly. The clock ticked, the windows throbbed and hammered in the gale. Presently she got up and went to the foot of the stairs. "Amelia!" she called, her voice cracking oddly.

There was no reply. She smiled and ran her thick tongue along her lips. She went up a few stairs and called again, then fetched a lighted candle from the drawing room and ascended to the first landing. "Amelia!" she called.

A sudden fierce gust of wind spurted down the passage and blew out the candle, leaving her in pitch darkness. She began to grope her way down the corridor, her fingers sliding along the wall. They came to a gap and she turned in to the left, moving forward till her thighs met a bed. "Amelia!" she called, and the echo was hurled hard back at her.

She moved across the room, her hands groping out before her, till they found another gap—the powder closet. This was crammed with her ancient and discarded clothes and stank of stale scent, sweat and decay. She touched a hanging frock and then another, her hands moving along. And then her right hand met something and she drew in her breath with a quickness.

The next second she was twisting and writhing and from her lips came a choked scream. As she was ruthlessly drawn in among the reeking stuffs, swinging wildly on their hooks, she struck out blindly with her clenched fists again and again. At last she leaned forward, buckling at the knees; her arms fell quivering to her sides. There was a long vile rattle from her throat, and she was still.

"It's a quarter past nine," said Clara. "Time you were off. You'd better have a drink before you go; it will help you to be firm, and you've got to be very firm." She poured out a stiff whisky which the Rector gulped down. Then he picked up his hat and coat and set out.

It had stopped raining, but it was still blowing a full gale and he had to fight his way against it. So soon as he entered the drive through the battered gates screeching on their hinges, he felt his nerves atingle. "As one who on a lonely road doth walk in fear and dread." The old lines leaped to his memory. He glanced fearfully up at the overhanging boughs. Was that a footstep close behind him? He broke into a run.

To his surprise he found the front door half open and went in. He saw a light in the drawing room, entered and found it empty. He waited a few moments and then called out timorously, "I'm here, Miss Pendleham!"

Before the echo of his voice died away, there came a long choked scream. "Good God, what was that!" he muttered, and sweat broke out on him. "It came from above. I must go up!"

He glanced distractedly around, picked up a candlestick, lit the candle and opened the door to the stairs with a quivering hand. As he hurried up the first flight, it seemed to him there was something astir in the house and that the shadows on the wall came from a company of persons following him up, and that others were awaiting him on the landing. He trembled and his breath came fast.

"Miss Pendleham!" he quavered. No sound. He lurched down the corridor till he came to an open door, through which he passed into a huge room. He raised the candlestick and peered fearfully about him. Ah, there was another door—open—and there was Miss Pendleham.

"Here I am, Miss Pendleham!" he said. What was she doing? He could only see her body from the waist down; the rest was buried in some clothes. He tiptoed into the closet and gingerly pulled the clothes aside. And then he sprang back with a clipped cry, for he was gazing into the battered, dead face of Amelia Lornon. She was leaning back against the wall, and she had drawn Miss Pendleham's head down on her breast. Her hands clutched her neck so fiercely and the nails were driven in so deep that the blood was seeping down over her lace collar.

The last shred of self-control left him. The candlestick fell from his hand, and he ran blunderingly from the room and down the stairs. The air seemed full of screams and laughter, something death-cold was pressed against his face, leaping figures ran beside him, till at last he staggered whimpering out into the night.

The Strange Valley

T. V. Olsen

The three horsemen came up on the brow of a hill, and the valley was below them. It was a broad cup filled by the brooding thickness of the prairie night. The light shed by a narrow sickle of moon picked out just another Dakota valley, about a mile across as the white men reckoned distance, and surrounded by a rim of treeless hills. The valley floor was covered by an ordinary growth of a few small oaks, a lot of brush, and some sandy flats with a sparse lacing of buffalo grass.

Young Elk said, "Is this what you wish us to see, Blue Goose?" He made no effort to keep the skepticism from his voice.

"Yes," said the rider on his left. "This is the place."

"Now that we're here, tell us again what you saw the other night." The third youth, the shaman's son, sounded very intent. "From where did it come?"

"From there." Blue Goose leaned forward as he pointed toward the eastern end of the valley. "As I told you, I'd had a long day of hunting, and I was very tired. I made my camp in the center of the valley, and fell asleep at once. This was about sunset.

"It was long after dark when I woke. I came awake all at once, and I don't know why. I heard a strange sound, a kind of growl that was very low and steady, and it was a long way off. But it was running very fast in my direction, and I sat in my blanket and waited."

Young Elk said with a grim smile, "Because you were too afraid even to run."

Blue Goose was silent for a moment. "Yes," he said honestly. "I was afraid. I didn't know what the thing was, but I knew it was getting closer. And growling louder all the while, as if in great pain or anger. Then I saw it.

"It was a huge beast, as big as a small hill, black in the night and running very close to the ground, and its two eyes were yellow and glaring. It went past me very close, but so fast I didn't think it saw me. It was bellowing as loud as a hundred bull buffaloes if they all bellowed at once. Suddenly it was gone."

"What do you mean, it was gone?" Young Elk demanded. "You said that before."

"I'm not sure. All I know is that suddenly I saw it no more and heard it no more."

"I wish you could tell us more about it," said the shaman's son. "But I suppose it was very dark."

"Yes," Blue Goose agreed. "Even a little darker than tonight." He hesitated. "I thought that the thing might be covered with scales—bright scales like a huge fish—since the moon seemed to glint on it here and there. But I couldn't be sure."

"You're not very sure of anything," Young Elk gibed.

Blue Goose sighed. "I do not know what I saw. As I have said, I left the valley very fast and camped a long way off that night. But I came back in the morning. I looked for the thing's spoor. I looked all over, and there was nothing. Yet I found where I had camped, and my pony's tracks and my own. But the thing left no sign at all."

"Because there had never been a thing. You should be more careful about what you eat, my friend." Young Elk spoke very soberly, though he felt like laughing out loud. "Spoiled meat in one's belly is like *mui waken*, the strong drink. It has a bad effect on the head."

For a little while the three young Sioux sat their ponies in silence, looking down into the dark stillness of the valley. A silky wind pressed up from the valley floor, a wind warm with the summer night and full of the ripening smells of late summer.

But something in it held a faint chill, and that was strange. Young Elk felt a crawl of gooseflesh on his bare shoulders, and he thought: *The night is turning cold, that is all.* He felt the nervous tremor run through his mount.

He laid his hand on the pony's shoulder and spoke quietly to the animal. He was angry at Blue

Goose, his best friend, for telling this foolish story and angry at himself for coming along tonight with the other two because he was deeply curious. And back in their camp only a few miles to the north there was firelight and laughter and a warm-eyed girl named Morning Teal, and Young Elk was a fool to be out here with his friend and with the son of that tired old faker of a medicine man.

Of late, Young Elk thought sourly, there had been more than the usual quota of wild stories of visions and bad spirits running rampant among the people. Early this same summer, on the river of the Greasy Grass that the whites called Little Big Horn, the long-haired General Custer had gone down to defeat and death with his troops. Many warriors of their own band had been among the twelve thousand Sioux, Cheyenne, and Arapaho who had helped in the annihilation of a hated enemy.

In the uneasy weeks since, as the people followed the buffalo, hunting and drying meat in the prospect of being driven back to the reservation by white cavalry, a rash of weird happenings were reported. Men who had died were seen walking the prairie with bloody arrows protruding from them. Voices of the dead were heard in the night wind. It was the shaman's part to encourage this sort of nonsense. A man claimed that a bluecoat soldier he had scalped appeared to him nightly with the blood still fresh on his head. The shaman chanted gibberish and told him to bury the scalp so that the ghost would trouble his nights no more.

Young Elk was disgusted. He had never seen

even one of these spirits. Only the fools who believed in such things ever saw them.

The shaman's son broke the long pause, speaking quietly. "This valley is a strange place. Today I spoke with my father and told him what Blue Goose has told us. He said that he knows of this place, and that his father's fathers knew of it too. Many strange things happened here in the old days. Men known to be long dead would be seen walking—not as spirits, but in the flesh. Still other things were seen, things too strange to be spoken of. Finally all our people of the Lakotas came to shun the valley. But that was so long ago that even most of the old ones have forgotten the stories."

Young Elk made a rude chuckling sound with his tongue and teeth.

"Young Elk does not believe in such things," the shaman's son observed. "Why then did he come with us tonight?"

"Because otherwise for the next moon I would hear nothing from you and Blue Goose but mad stories about what you saw tonight. I'd prefer to see it for myself."

"Oh," said Blue Goose, "then there *was* something? I did not make this great story out of the air?"

"Maybe not." Young Elk said slyly, "Maybe it was the white man's iron horse that Blue Goose saw."

"Now you jest with me. Even though I am not all-wise like Young Elk, still I know that the iron horse of the *wasicun* runs on two shining rails, and there are no rails here. And the iron horse does not growl thus, nor does it have two eyes that flame in the dark."

Another silence stretched among the three youths as they sat their ponies on the crest of the hill and peered down into the dark valley. And Young Elk thought angrily, *What is this?* They had come here to go down in the valley and wait in the night, in hopes that the thing Blue Goose had seen would make another appearance. Yet they all continued to sit here as though a winter of the spirit had descended and frozen them all to the spot.

Young Elk gave a rough laugh. "Come on!" He kneed his pony forward, down the long grassy dip of hill. The others followed.

Near the bottom, Young Elk's pony turned suddenly skittish, and he had to fight the shying animal to bring him under control. Blue Goose and the shaman's son were having trouble with their mounts too.

"This is a bad omen," panted the shaman's son. "Maybe we had better go back."

"No," Young Elk said angrily, for his pony's behavior and the strange feeling of the place were putting an edge on his temper. "We've come this far, and now we'll see what there is to see, if anything. Where was Blue Goose when he thought he saw the beast?"

Blue Goose said, "We must go this way," and forced his horse through a heavy tangle of choke-cherry brush. He led the way very quickly, as though afraid that his nerve would not hold much longer.

They came to a rather open stretch of sand flats

that caught a pale glimmer of moonglow; it was studded with clumps of thicket and a few scrub oaks. "Here is the place," Blue Goose told them.

The three Sioux settled down to wait. Nobody suggested that it would be more comfortable to dismount. Somehow it seemed better to remain on their ponies and accept a cramp or two. It was only, Young Elk told himself, that they should be ready for anything, and they might have a sudden need of the ponies.

Once more it was the shaman's son who ended an interval of silence. "What time of the night did it happen, Blue Goose?"

"I can't be sure. But close to this time, I think."

Silence again. The ponies shuffled nervously. The wind hushed through some dead brush, which rattled like dry, hollow bird bones. Idly Young Elk slipped his throwing-ax from his belt and toyed with it. He slid his hand over the familiar shape of the flint head and the fresh thongs of green rawhide that lashed it to the new handle he had put on only this morning. His palm felt moist.

And his head felt slightly dizzy. Now the shapes of rocks, the black masses of brush, seemed to shimmer and swim; the landscape seemed misty and unreal as if seen through a veil of fog, yet there was no fog. *It is a trick of the moon,* Young Elk thought. He gripped the ax tighter; his knuckles began to ache.

"There!" Blue Goose whispered. "Do you hear it?"

Young Elk snapped, "I hear the wind," but even

as the words formed on his lips the sound was increasing, unmistakably not the wind. Not even a gale wind roaring through the treetops of a great forest made such a noise. As yet he could see nothing, but he knew that the sound was moving in their direction.

Suddenly the two yellow eyes of which Blue Goose had spoken came boring out of the night. Now he could see the hulking black shape of the monster running toward them at an incredible speed and so low to the ground that its legs could not be seen. All the while the strange humming roar it made was steadily growing.

The ponies were plunging and rearing with fear. The shaman's son gave a cry of pure panic and achieved enough control over his mount to kick it into a run. In a moment Blue Goose bolted after him.

Young Elk fought his terrified pony down and held the trembling animal steady, his own fear swallowed in an eagerness to have a closer look at the thing. But he was not prepared for the fury of its rush as it bore down toward him. And its round, glaring eyes blinded him—he could see nothing beyond them.

It let out a piercing, horrible shriek as it neared him—it was hardly the length of three ponies away—and it seemed to hesitate. It hissed at him, a long gushing hiss, while the yellow eyes bathed him in their wicked glare.

Young Elk waited no longer. He lunged his pony in an angling run that carried him past the thing's blunt snout, and in that moment brought his arm back and flung the ax with all his strength. He heard it make a strange hollow boom, although he did not see it hit, and then he was racing on through the brush, straining low to his pony's withers, heedless of the tearing branches.

Young Elk did not slow down till he reached the end of the valley; then he looked back without stopping. There was no sign of the beast. The valley was deserted and quiet under the dim moonlight.

Young Elk crossed the rim of hills and caught up with his friends on the prairie beyond. "Did you see it?" the shaman's son demanded eagerly.

"No. Its eyes blinded me. But I hit it with my ax." Young Elk paused; his heart was pounding so fiercely in his chest he was afraid they would hear it, so he went quickly on, "I heard the ax hit the thing. So it was not a ghost."

"How do you know?" countered the shaman's son. "Where did it go? Did you see?"

"No," Young Elk said bitterly. "It was very fast."

"Let's go back to camp," Blue Goose said. "I don't care what the thing was. I do not want to think about it."

Joe Kercheval had been dozing in his seat when his partner, Johnny Antelope, hit the brakes of the big truck and gave Joe a bad jolt. And then Joe nearly blew his stack when Johnny told him the reason he had slammed to an abrupt stop on this long, lonely highway in the middle of nowhere.

"I tell you, I saw him," Johnny insisted as he

started up again and drove on. "A real old-time Sioux buck on a spotted pony. He was sitting on his nag right in the middle of the road, and I almost didn't stop in time. Then he came charging past the cab, and I saw him fling something—I think it was an ax—at the truck. I heard it hit. You were waking up just then—you must have heard it."

"I heard a rock thrown up by the wheels hit somewheres against the trailer, that's all," Joe said flatly. "You been on the road too long, kid. You ought to lay off a few weeks, spend a little time with your relatives on the reservation."

Johnny Antelope shook his head. "I saw him, Joe. And then I didn't see him. I mean—I could swear he disappeared—simply vanished into thin air—just as he rode past the cab. Of course it was pretty dark . . ."

"Come off it. For a college-educated Indian, you get some pretty far-out notions. I've made this run a hundred times and I never seen any wild redskins with axes, spooks or for real."

"You white men don't know it all, Joe. You're Johnny-come-latelies. This has been our country for a long, long time, and I could tell you some things . . . " Johnny paused, squinting through the windshield at the racing ribbon of highway unfolding in the tunneling brightness of the headlights. "I was just remembering. This is a stretch of land the Sioux have always shunned. There are all kinds of legends concerning it. I remember one story in particular my old granddaddy used to tell us kids— I guess he told it a hundred times or more . . ."

"Nuts on your granddaddy."

Johnny Antelope smiled. "Maybe you're right, at that. Old Blue Goose always did have quite an imagination."

"So does his grandson." Joe Kercheval cracked his knuckles. "There's a turnoff just up ahead, kid. Swing around there."

"What for, Joe?"

"We're going back to where you seen that wild man on a horse. I'm gonna prove to you all you seen was moonshine." Joe paused, then added wryly, "Seems like I got to prove it to myself, too. I say it was just a rock that hit the truck, and I'll be losin' sleep if I don't find out for sure."

Without another word Johnny swung the big truck around and headed back east on the highway. The two truckers were silent until Johnny slowed and brought the truck to a shrieking stop. The air brakes were still hissing as he leaned from the window, pointing. "Here's the spot, Joe. I recognize that twisted oak on the right."

"Okay, let's have a close look." They climbed out of the cab, and Johnny pointed out the exact spot where he had first seen the Indian warrior, and where the warrior had cut off the highway alongside the cab and thrown his ax.

"Look here, kid." Joe played his flashlight beam over the roadside. "Soft shoulders. If your boy left the concrete right here, his horse would of tromped some mighty deep prints in the ground. Not a sign, see?"

"Wait a minute," Johnny Antelope said. "Flash

that torch over here, Joe." He stooped and picked up something from the sandy shoulder.

The halo of light touched the thing Johnny held in his outstretched hand. "Know what this is, Joe?" he asked softly. "A Sioux throwing-ax."

Joe swallowed. He started to snort, "Nuts. So it's an ax . . . " but the words died on his lips.

For under the flashlight beam, even as the two men watched, the wooden handle of the ax was dissolving into rotted punk, and the leather fastenings were turning cracked and brittle, crumbling away. Only the stone blade remained in Johnny's hand, as old and flinty and weathered as if it had lain there by the road for an untold number of years. . . .

The Christmas Spirit

Dorothy B. Bennett

It was a magazine of short stories, and an evil odor
came from it; from specific pages of it, as I found
when I flicked through them. I couldn't think why
anyone would buy such a collection of bizarre,
gruesome stories: tales of mystery, horror, rape,
torture, vampires and things that go plop in the
night. I wouldn't—even in ordinary circumstances,
let alone as I was now, in sole charge of the Emergency Ward at night at the Cottage Hospital.

Not long out of student class, I felt much less
than competent or confident. Frankly, I was all of
a jitter, especially since the hospital was on a skel-
eton staff, and half of those were at the Council
Chamber rehearsing for the show they were to put
on in the wards tomorrow, Christmas Day.

So, this Christmas Eve the ward was quiet and
somber and I wished I had a part in the play that

would have taken me out of there, but nobody thought of junior nurses as actresses. Nervously I listened to the breathing, often labored, of my patients, and sat where I'd found the magazine, at the table at the end of the ward under a dim bulb.

I flipped through the pages and wrinkled my nose in disgust. I sprayed my nose and mouth, for it was an odor of death, decay, putrefaction: an evil, abominable smell. Maybe Joyce, the day nurse, had borrowed it from her fiancé the mortuary attendant, for he had a morbid temperament; but it should have been treated before coming into the wards, especially this one, the Emergency, where there were open wounds without the benefit of safeguarding scar tissue yet.

Even as I thought of this, Joyce, having discarded uniform in favor of civvies, put her head round the door: "I'm off to the Council Chamber, Helen. I found the magazine in Number Ten's locker. It stinks, so I threw it out. 'Bye now, don't do anything I haven't had the chance to do."

The magazine was that month's issue. A monthly, date December 20th, four days ago. I finally decided that the smell came from one story: "Oriental Conceptions." Birth control, I thought at first, but soon saw that it was concerned with ancient deities, black arts, voodoo rites, how to invoke the aid of the gods. A chapter about charms, amulets, incantations, curses, spells. In between the pages of this yarn I found what I took to be a dried leaf, but of a type I'd never seen before.

Occasionally I put down the book to tiptoe along

the ward, expecting to find under every bed a spirit, elemental or supernatural being; for the book had impressed me more than I would have thought possible. I felt strange vibrations, an aura in the air of expectancy.

The next chapter was about Black Magic, rites and ceremonies often conducted in the wild places of the world by witch doctors and medicine men: how to throw curses and cast spells. I put the book down and shivered. I wanted nothing to do with spells here, where Death waited at each bedside. I sniffed my hands again and my stomach heaved. At the sluice I drenched myself in deodorants and stood a minute in the comparatively fresh air of the corridor. A passing porter said: "Good evening, Nurse Helen. Phew, you smell like Death warmed up and gone rotten. Who've you been with?"

Back in the ward the magazine seemed to draw me. I noticed that the story was in the first person, the writer a Djala Svenburt. I remembered that was the name of Number Ten. An uncommon name, must be the same man. From what I'd read, the author was a doctor, skilled in the ways of the West, who'd "gone native": gone to the East to study their methods—and finally decided they were as good and maybe in some ways better than ours. He'd studied their medical know-how and was lecturing on the subject back here.

So far I'd only glanced at the "case card" at the head of his bed, for he seemed to be sleeping soundly and his breathing was normal. I read his card again. Traffic accident; suspected internal injuries; await consultant's advice before further treatment. Under heavy sedation. He was a small, dark man, deep-set eyes, sunken cheeks. Normally Joyce would have given particulars of any new case before she left me, but in the excitement of the Christmas preparations this had been forgotten.

Anyway, he seemed peaceful enough. I hoped he'd remain that way, for there wasn't much of him; he looked as if a whisper from Death would entice him away.

Brisk footsteps at the doorway and I turned to see Dr. Kafter, our consultant. I'd seen him several times previously, but of course he was much too important to have seen me, a mere nurse. He didn't now; merely stooped from his great height to read the case card of Number Ten. Dr. Kafter was the bane of the doctors and nurses, even the Matron. A dominant, sardonic, sarcastic, bullying man.

"Ah, that's the man I've been summoned to see. Svenburt. Asleep, I see. Svenburt, charlatan, lecturer, writer, advocate of Black Magic, native drugs and medicines. Well, nurse, since the house surgeon hasn't had the common decency to wait for me, but has gone off to some idiotic Christmas festivity, what have you to tell me about this man? Nothing except what is on this card, I suppose? Ah, I thought so. Such inefficiency. I'll see that word of this gets to the proper authorities. Let me see what modern traffic has done to the specialist 'gone native.' "

He threw back the bedclothes and made a brief but expert examination. Straightening up and holding his back, he grunted: "Not much wrong. Should be out and about in a few days. Pity. I'd expected that he would have ruined his constitution by indulging in prehistoric rites. What's that book you have?"

I'd forgotten that I'd laid it at the foot of the bed. He snatched it up. It opened out for him at the page I'd been reading. He sniffed, gulped, glanced through it, skipping from page to page.

"Lot of rubbish . . . Balderdash! Nonsense and humbug! Mumbo jumbo from the mists of antiquity. What's the horrible smell?"

"It seems to come from that dead leaf stuck in the pages, sir."

He plucked out the leaf. The pulp of flesh had dried away, leaving a stringy network of veins.

"Dead leaf, girl? Dead leaf? This isn't a dead leaf. It's a bat wing. The wing of a long-dead bat. Skeletal membranes. The wing of a certain type of vampire bat. This fool and people like him believe that so long as this wing is impressed or imprisoned in any of their possessions, so long will life remain in their body. A relic of paganism."

With a quick jerk of his wrist he flipped the bat wing away, pushed the magazine at me and stalked out, calling out: "I'll call in at the Council Chamber to tell them what I think of them for leaving the hospital practically unattended."

The bat wing had not yet reached the ground. I watched it, mesmerized, for it fluttered like a wounded bird, gliding from side to side but ever downward although striving to regain height. It came to rest at my feet and I jumped back, for it still fluttered and convulsed and rolled as if in agony. There was a small shriek from Number Ten, a strangled gasp as he sat up in bed and then dropped back. I sprang to his side. No breathing, no pulse. I applied the usual tests, but he was dead.

Rushing to the window in the corridor, I saw Dr. Kafter getting into his car and called to him. Reading my panic aright, he bounded upstairs.

"He's dead," I said. "Mr. Svenburt. Number Ten."

"Don't be foolish, girl," he snarled, as he bent over the figure in the bed. His brows knitted and he shook his head as he shouted to me: "Oxygen." I was already at his side with it. Most of the ward were now awake. Dr. Kafter pushed the oxygen apparatus at me and rushed out for his bag. The oxygen did not revive the patient, nor did the other remedies Dr. Kafter applied.

"That's a double dose, but don't ever tell anybody that," he said as he withdrew a syringe. "If that doesn't fetch him back, nothing ever will."

But it didn't. Five minutes later he signed a death certificate.

"That leaf, sir?" I questioned. "I mean, the dead bat wing? Could that have anything to do with his death?"

"Don't be ridiculous. Pure superstition. Every country, tribe, religion, have their superstitions, all without power. Where is that bat wing?"

It wasn't where it had fallen. We made a brief search, but couldn't find it. "No matter," Dr. Kafter said. "It couldn't help him, now, even if once it could; and only ignorant fools could ever believe that."

I watched him drive away, soothed and calmed down my patients, dispensed sleeping tablets and soon had the ward quiet again—but not entirely silent. There was an awful feeling of unease about, and what I could only describe to myself as a "jungle smell": a muggy miasma.

After a while I found myself listening to a scrabbling sound. Mice? Not in this hospital. A patient, half asleep, scratching himself? I listened at each bed. At the last bed, in the corner, I felt warm, for the scratching sounded nearer. Then I was cold, for the bat wing was struggling in the corner. Fluttering! Or were stray puffs of wind moving it? I shut the door. Still it strived.

Remembering the magazine, I retrieved it from under Number Ten bed, took it to that corner. Then I did the bravest thing I have ever done: gently picked up that fluttering "leaf," cupped it tenderly in my hands and transferred it to its original place in the book. It immediately relaxed like a tired baby placed in its cot. As I did so there was a great sigh from Number Ten. The eyelids fluttered and the lips moved. I forgot all our up-to-date resuscitation methods and applied the Kiss of Life.

Was there anything in those ancient beliefs? One breathing Life into a dead body two thousand years ago was a legend disbelieved by most until this ancient practice had been tried again and found successful.

Svenburt was again breathing, evenly and serenely. His eyes opened, and full consciousness was there. He even smiled at me, sedation overcome and Death defeated. His eyes were upon the locker at his side, staring at a rabbit's foot there. I remembered then that Dr. Kafter had pulled it from his pocket when he spoke of every country, tribe, religion having their own superstitions. So this was his personal superstition: a rabbit's foot for good luck. He'd put it down as we looked for the bat wing. Had he forgotten it, or deliberately left it there to show his disregard for superstition?

Anyway, I'd have to inform Dr. Kafter that the patient he'd certified dead was very much alive. In fact, sitting up and smiling at me—the magazine in his hand. "My talisman," he observed, opening the pages to show the dead "leaf."

I phoned the Council Chamber, asked for the consultant. Joyce came to the phone. "You can't speak to Dr. Kafter—unless you go to Hell to do it. He died within a minute of getting here. Heart, I expect."

That would be at about the time that Number Ten took on a new lease of life. Any connection? A swap by the Controller, ancient and modern?

Very thoughtfully, I went back to the ward.

Mr. Svenburt was fingering the rabbit's foot. "Somebody left this on my locker. That means a bad spell for him. Can I have my clothes please? Life is calling."

The Bronze Door

Raymond Chandler

The little man was from the Calabar coast or from
Papua or Tongatabu, some such remote place like
that. An empire builder frayed at the temples, thin
and yellow, and slightly drunk at the club bar. And
he was wearing a faded school tie he had probably
kept year after year in a tin box so the centipedes
wouldn't eat it.

Mr. Sutton-Cornish didn't know him, at least not
then, but he knew the tie because it was his own
school tie. So he spoke to the man timidly, and the
man talked to him, being a little drunk and not
knowing anybody. They had drinks and talked of
the old school, in that peculiar, remote way the
English have, without exchanging names, but
friendly underneath.

It was a big thrill for Mr. Sutton-Cornish, because
nobody ever talked to him at the club except the

servants. He was too ingrowing, and you don't have to talk to people in London clubs. That's what they're for.

Mr. Sutton-Cornish got home to tea a little thick-tongued, for the first time in fifteen years. He sat there blankly in the upstairs drawing room, holding his cup of tepid tea and going over the man's face in his mind, making it younger and chubbier, a face that would go over an Eton collar or under a school cricket cap.

Suddenly he got it, and chuckled. That was something he hadn't done in a good few years either.

"Llewellyn, m'dear," he said. "Llewellyn Minor. Had an elder brother. Killed in the War, in the horse artillery."

Mrs. Sutton-Cornish stared at him bleakly across the heavily embroidered tea cozy. Her chestnut-colored eyes were dull with disdain—dried-out chestnuts, not fresh ones. The rest of her large face looked gray. The late October afternoon was gray, and the heavy, full-bottomed, monogramed curtains across the windows. Even the ancestors on the walls were gray—all except the bad one, the general.

The chuckle died in Mr. Sutton-Cornish's throat. The long gray stare took care of that. Then he shivered a little, and as he wasn't very steady, his hand jerked. He emptied his tea on the rug, almost delicately, cup and all.

"Oh, rot," he said thickly. "Sorry, m'dear. Missed me trousers, though. Awfully sorry, m'dear."

For a minute Mrs. Sutton-Cornish made only the

sound of a large woman breathing. Then suddenly things began to tinkle on her—to tinkle and rustle and squeak. She was full of quaint noises, like a haunted house, but Mr. Sutton-Cornish shuddered, because he knew she was trembling with rage.

"Ah-h-h," she breathed out very, very slowly, after a long time, in her firing-squad manner. "Ah-h-h. Intoxicated, James?"

Something stirred suddenly at her feet. Teddy, the Pomeranian, stopped snoring and lifted his head and smelled blood. He let out a short snapping bark, merely a ranging shot, and waddled to his feet. His protuberant brown eyes stared malignantly at Mr. Sutton-Cornish.

"I'd better ring the bell, m'dear," Mr. Sutton-Cornish said humbly, and stood up. "Hadn't I?"

She didn't answer him. She spoke to Teddy instead, softly. A sort of doughy softness, with something sadistic in it.

"Teddy," she said softly, "look at that man. Look at that man, Teddy."

Mr. Sutton-Cornish said thickly: "Now don't let him snap at me, m'dear. D-don't let him snap at me, please, m'dear."

No answer. Teddy braced himself and leered. Mr. Sutton-Cornish tore his eyes away and looked up at the bad ancestor, the general. The general wore a scarlet coat with a diagonal blue sash across it, rather like a bar sinister. He had the flushed complexion generals used to have in his day. He had a lot of very fruity-looking decorations and a bold stare, the stare of an unrepentant sinner. The general was no violet. He had broken up more homes than he had fought duels, and he had fought more duels than he had won battles, and he had won plenty of battles.

Looking up at the bold-veined face, Mr. Sutton-Cornish braced himself, leaned down and took a small triangular sandwich from the tea table.

"Here, Teddy," he gulped. "Catch, boy, catch!"

He threw the sandwich. It fell in front of Teddy's little brown paws. Teddy snuffled it languidly and yawned. He had his meals served to him on china, not thrown at him. He sidled innocently over to the edge of the rug and suddenly pounced on it, snarling.

"At table, James?" Mrs. Sutton-Cornish said slowly and dreadfully.

Mr. Sutton-Cornish stood on his teacup. It broke into thin light slivers of fine china. He shuddered again.

But now was the time. He started quickly towards the bell. Teddy let him get almost there, still pretending to worry the fringe of the rug. Then he spat out a piece of fringe, and charged low and soundlessly, his small feet like feathers in the nap of the rug. Mr. Sutton-Cornish was just reaching for the bell.

Small bright teeth tore rapidly and expertly at a pearl-gray spat.

Mr. Sutton-Cornish yelped, pivoted swiftly—and

kicked. His neat shoe flashed in the gray light. A silky brown object sailed through the air and landed gobbling.

Then there was a quite indescribable stillness in the room, like the silence in the innermost room of a cold-storage warehouse, at midnight.

Teddy whimpered once, artfully, crept along the floor with his body close to it, crept under Mrs. Sutton-Cornish's chair. Her purplish-brown skirts moved and Teddy's face emerged slowly, framed in silk, the face of a nasty old woman with a shawl over her head.

"Caught me off balance," Mr. Sutton-Cornish mumbled, leaning against the mantelpiece. "Didn't mean . . . never intended—"

Mrs. Sutton-Cornish rose. She rose with the air of gathering a retinue about her. Her voice was the cold bleat of a foghorn on an icy river.

"Chinverly," she said. "I shall leave at once for Chinverly. At once. This hour . . . Drunk! Filthily drunk in the middle of the afternoon. Kicking little inoffensive animals. Vile! Utterly vile! *Open the door!*"

Mr. Sutton-Cornish staggered across the room and opened the door. She went out. Teddy trotted beside her, on the side away from Mr. Sutton-Cornish, and for once he didn't try to trip her in the doorway.

Outside she turned, slowly, as a liner turns.

"James," she said, "have you anything to say to me?"

He giggled—from pure nervous strain.

She looked at him horribly, turned again, said

over her shoulder: "This is the end, James. The end of our marriage."

Mr. Sutton-Cornish said appallingly: "Goodness, m'dear—are we married?"

She started to turn again, but didn't. A sound like somebody being strangled in a dungeon came from her. Then she went on.

The door of the room hung open like a paralyzed mouth. Mr. Sutton-Cornish stood just inside it, listening. He didn't move until he heard steps on the floor above—heavy steps—hers. He sighed and looked down at his torn spat. Then he crept downstairs, into his long, narrow study beside the entrance hall, and got at the whisky.

He hardly noticed the sounds of departure, luggage being descended, voices, the throbbing of the big car out in front, voices, the last bark from Teddy's iron-old throat. The house grew utterly silent. The furniture waited with its tongue in its cheek. Outside the lamps were lit in a light fog. Taxis hooted along the wet street. The fire died low in the grate.

Mr. Sutton-Cornish stood in front of it, swaying a little, looking at his long gray face in the wall mirror.

"Take a little stroll," he whispered wryly. "You and me. Never was anyone else, was there?"

He sneaked out into the hall without Collins, the butler, hearing him. He got his scarf and overcoat and hat on, grasped his stick and gloves, let himself out silently into the dusk.

He stood a little while at the bottom of the steps

and looked up at the house. No. 14 Grinling Crescent. His father's house, his grandfather's house, his great-grandfather's house. All he had left. The rest was hers. Even the clothes he wore, the money in his bank account. But the house was still his—at least in name.

Four white steps, as spotless as the souls of virgins, leading up to an apple-green, deep-paneled door, painted as things used to be painted long ago, in the age of leisure. It had a brass knocker and a thumb latch above the handle and one of those bells you twisted, instead of pushing or pulling them, and it rang just on the other side of the door, rather ridiculously, if you were not used to it.

He turned and looked across the street at the little railed-in park always kept locked, where on sunny days the small, prim children of Grinling Crescent walked along the smooth paths, around the little ornamental lake, beside the rhododendron bushes, holding the hands of their nursemaids.

He looked at all this a little wanly, then he squared his thin shoulders and marched off into the dusk, thinking of Nairobi and Papua and Tongatabu, thinking of the man in the faded school tie who would go back there presently, wherever it was he came from, and lie awake in the jungle, thinking of London.

"Keb, sir?"

Mr. Sutton-Cornish halted, stood on the edge of the curb and stared. The voice came from above, one of those wind-husked, beery voices you don't hear very often anymore. It came from the driver's seat of a hansom cab.

The hansom cab had come out of the darkness, sliding oilily along the street on high rubber-tired wheels, the horse's hoofs making a slow, even *clop-clop* that Mr. Sutton-Cornish hadn't noticed until the driver called down to him.

It looked real enough. The horse had time-worn black blinkers and the characteristic well-fed and yet somehow dilapidated look that cab horses used to have. The half doors of the hansom were folded back and Mr. Sutton-Cornish could see the quilted gray upholstery inside. The long reins were riddled with cracks, and following them upward he saw the beefy driver, the wide-brimmed coachman's "topper" he wore, the huge buttons on the upper part of his greatcoat and the well-worn blanket that swathed the lower part of him round and round. He held his long whip lightly and delicately, as a hansom driver should hold his whip.

The trouble was that there weren't any more hansom cabs.

Mr. Sutton-Cornish gulped, slipped a glove off and reached out to touch the wheel. It was very cold, very solid, wet with the muddy slime of the city streets.

"Doubt if I've ever seen one of these since the War," he said out loud, very steadily.

"Wot war, guv'nor?"

Mr. Sutton-Cornish started. He touched the wheel again. Then he smiled, slowly and carefully drew his glove on again.

"I'm getting in," he said.

"Steady there, Prince," the driver wheezed.

The horse switched his long tail contemptuously. Telling *him* to be steady. Mr. Sutton-Cornish climbed in over the wheel, rather clumsily, because one had lost the knack of that art these many years. He closed the half doors around in front of him, leaned back against the seat in the pleasant harness-room smell.

The trap opened over his head and the driver's large nose and alcoholic eyes made an improbable picture in the opening, like a deep-sea fish staring you down through the glass wall of an aquarium.

"Where to, guv'nor?"

"Well . . . Soho." It was the most foreign place he could think of—for a hansom cab to go to.

.The cabman's eyes stared down at him.

"Won't like it there, guv'nor."

"I don't have to like it," Mr. Sutton-Cornish said bitterly.

The cabman stared down at him a little longer. "Yus," he said. "Soho. Wardour Street like. Right you are, guv'nor."

The trap slammed shut, the whip flicked delicately beside the horse's right ear and motion came to the hansom cab.

Mr. Sutton-Cornish sat perfectly still, his scarf tight around his thin neck and his stick between his knees and his gloved hands clasped on the crook of the stick. He stared mutely out into the mist, like an animal on the bridge. The horse *clop-clopped* out of Grinling Crescent, through Belgrave Square, over to Whitehall, up to Trafalgar Square, across that to St. Martin's Lane.

It went neither fast nor slow, and yet it went as fast as anything else went. It moved without sound, except for the *clop-clop*, across a world that stank of gasoline fumes, and charred oil, that shrilled with whistles and hooted with horns.

And nobody seemed to notice it and nothing seemed to get in its way. That was rather amazing, Mr. Sutton-Cornish thought. But after all, a hansom cab had nothing to do with that world. It was a ghost, an underlayer of time, the first writing on a palimpsest, brought out by ultraviolet light in a darkened room.

"Y'know," he said, speaking to the horse's rump, because there wasn't anything else there to speak to, "things might happen to a man, if a man would just let them happen."

The long whip flicked by Prince's ear as lightly as a trout fly flicking at a small dark pool under a rock.

"They already have," he added glumly.

The cab slowed along a curb, and the trap snapped open again.

"Well, 'ere we are, guv'nor. 'Ow about one of them little French dinners for eighteen pence? You know, guv'nor. Six courses of nothink at all. You 'ave one on me and then I 'ave one on you and we're still 'ungry. 'Ow about it?"

A very chill hand clutched at Mr. Sutton-

Cornish's heart. Six-course dinners for eighteen pence? A hansom-cab driver who said: "Wot war, guv'nor?" Twenty years ago, perhaps—

"Let me out here!" he said shrilly.

He threw the doors open, thrust money up at the face in the trap, hopped over the wheel to the sidewalk.

He didn't quite run, but he walked pretty fast and close to a dark wall and a little slinkingly. But nothing followed him, not even the *clop-clop* of the horse's hoofs. He swung around a corner into a narrow crowded street.

The light came from the open door of a shop. CURIOS AND ANTIQUES, it said on the façade, in letters once gold, heavily Gothic in style. There was a flare on the sidewalk to attract attention and by this light he read the sign. The voice came from inside, from a little, plump man standing on a box who chanted over the heads of a listless crowd of silent, bored, foreign-looking men. The chanting voice held a note of exhaustion and futility.

"Now what am I bid, gents? Now what am I bid on this magnificent example of Oriental art? One pound starts the ball rolling, gents. One pound note, coin of the realm. Now 'oo says a pound, gents? 'Oo says a pound?"

Nobody said anything. The little plump man on the box shook his head, wiped his face with a dirty handkerchief and drew a long breath. Then he saw Mr. Sutton-Cornish standing on the fringe of the little crowd.

"'Ow about you, sir?" he pounced. "You look as

if you'd a country 'ouse. Now that door's made for a country 'ouse. 'Ow about you, sir? Just give me a start like."

Mr. Sutton-Cornish blinked at him. "Eh? What's that?" he snapped.

The listless men smiled faintly and spoke among themselves without moving their thick lips.

"No offense, sir," the auctioneer chirped. "If you did 'ave a country 'ouse, that there door might be just what you could use."

Mr. Sutton-Cornish turned his head slowly, following the auctioneer's pointing hand, and looked for the first time at the bronze door.

It stood all by itself over against the left-hand wall of the nearly stripped shop. It stood about two feet from the side wall, on its own base. It was a double door, apparently of cast bronze, although from its size that seemed impossible. It was heavily scrolled over with a welter of Arabic script in relief, an endless story that here found no listener, a procession of curves and dots that might have expressed anything from an anthology of the Koran to the bylaws of a well-organized harem.

The two leaves of the door were only part of the thing. It had a wide, heavy base below and a superstructure topped by a Moorish arch. From the meeting edge of the two leaves a huge key stuck out of a huge keyhole, the sort of key a medieval jailer used to wear in enormous clanking bunches on a leather belt around his waist. A key from *The Yeomen of the Guard*—a comic-opera key.

"Oh . . . that," Mr. Sutton-Cornish said in the

stillness. "Well, really, you know. I'm afraid not that, you know."

The auctioneer sighed. No hope had ever been smaller, probably, but at least it was worth a sigh. Then he picked up something which might have been carved ivory, but wasn't, stared at it pessimistically and burst out again:

"Now 'ere, gents, I 'old in my 'and one of the finest examples—"

Mr. Sutton-Cornish smiled faintly and skimmed along the cluster of men until he came close to the bronze door.

He stood in front of it leaning on his stick, which was a section of polished rhinoceros hide over a steel core, dull mahogany in color, and a stick even a heavy man could have leaned on. After a while he reached forward idly and twisted the great key. It turned stubbornly, but it turned. A ring beside it was the doorknob. He twisted that, too, and tugged one half of the door open.

He straightened, and with a pleasantly idle gesture thrust his stick forward through the opening. And then, for the second time that evening, something incredible happened to him.

He wheeled sharply. Nobody was paying any attention. The auction was dead on its feet. The silent men were drifting out into the night. In a pause, hammering sounded at the back of the shop. The plump little auctioneer looked more and more as if he were eating a bad egg.

Mr. Sutton-Cornish looked down at his gloved right hand. There was no stick in it. There was nothing in it. He stepped to one side and looked behind the door. There was no stick there, on the dusty floor.

He had felt nothing. Nothing had jerked him. The stick had merely passed partway through the door and then—it had merely ceased to exist.

He leaned down and picked up a piece of torn paper, wadded it swiftly into a ball, glanced behind him again and tossed the ball through the open part of the door.

Then he let out a slow sigh in which some neolithic rapture struggled with his civilized amazement. The ball of paper didn't fall to the floor behind the door. It fell, in midair, clean out of the visible world.

Mr. Sutton-Cornish reached his empty right hand forward and very slowly and carefully pushed the door shut. Then he just stood there, and licked his lips.

After a while: "Harem door," he said very softly. "Exit door of a harem. Now, that's an idea."

A very charming idea, too. The silken lady, her night of pleasure with the sultan over, would be conducted politely to that door and would casually step through it. Then nothing. No sobbing in the night, no broken hearts, no blackamoor with cruel eyes and a large scimitar, no knotted silk cord, no blood, no dull splash in the midnight Bosphorus. Merely nothing. A cool, clean, perfectly timed and perfectly irrevocable absence of existence. Someone would close the door and lock it and take the key out, and for the time being that would be that.

Mr. Sutton-Cornish didn't notice the emptying of the shop. Faintly he heard its street door close, but without giving it any meaning. The hammering at the back stopped for a moment, voices spoke. Then steps came near. They were weary steps in the silence, the steps of a man who had had enough of that day, and of many such days. A voice spoke at Mr. Sutton-Cornish's elbow, an end-of-the-day voice.

"A very fine piece of work, sir. A bit out of my line—to be frank."

Mr. Sutton-Cornish didn't look at him, not yet. "Quite a bit out of anybody's line," he said gravely.

"I see it interests you, sir, after all."

Mr. Sutton-Cornish turned his head slowly. Down on the floor, off his box, the auctioneer was a mere wisp of a man. A shabby, unpressed, red-eyed little man who had found life no picnic.

"Yes, but what would one *do* with it?" Mr. Sutton-Cornish asked throatily.

"Well—it's a door like any other, sir. Bit 'eavy. Bit queer-like. But still a door like any other."

"I wonder," Mr. Sutton-Cornish said, still throatily.

The auctioneer gave him a swift appraising glance, shrugged and gave it up. He sat down on an empty box, lit a cigarette and relaxed sloppily into private life.

"What are you asking for it?" Mr. Sutton-Cornish inquired, quite suddenly. "What are you asking for it, Mr.—"

"Skimp, sir. Josiah Skimp. Well, a twenty-pound

note, sir? Bronze alone ought to be worth that for artwork." The little man's eyes were glittering again.

Mr. Sutton-Cornish nodded absently. "I don't know much about that."

" 'Ell of a lot of it, sir." Mr. Skimp hopped off his box, patted over and heaved the leaf of the door open, grunting. "Beats me 'ow it ever got 'ere. For seven-footers. No door for shrimps like me. Look, sir."

Mr. Sutton-Cornish had a rather ghastly presentiment, of course. But he didn't do anything about it. He couldn't. His tongue stuck in his throat and his legs were like ice. The comical contrast between the massiveness of the door and his own wisp of a body seemed to amuse Mr. Skimp. His little, round face threw back the shadow of a grin. Then he lifted his foot and hopped.

Mr. Sutton-Cornish watched him—as long as there was anything to watch. In fact he watched much longer. The hammering at the back of the shop seemed to get quite thunderous in the silence.

Once more, after a long time, Mr. Sutton-Cornish bent forward and closed the door. This time he twisted the key and dragged it out and put it in his overcoat pocket.

"Got to do something," he mumbled. "Got to do— Can't let this sort of thing—" His voice trailed off and then he jerked violently, as though a sharp pain had shot through him. Then he laughed out loud, off key. Not a natural laugh. Not a very nice laugh.

"That was beastly," he said under his breath. "But amazingly funny."

He was still standing there rooted when a pale young man with a hammer appeared at his elbow.

"Mr. Skimp step out, sir—or did you notice? We're supposed to be closed up, sir."

Mr. Sutton-Cornish didn't look up at the pale young man with the hammer. Moving a clammy tongue, he said:

"Yes . . . Mr. Skimp . . . stepped out."

The young man started to turn away. Mr. Sutton-Cornish made a gesture. "I've bought this door—from Mr. Skimp," he said. "Twenty pounds. Will you take the money—and my card?"

The pale young man beamed, delighted at personal contact with a sale. Mr. Sutton-Cornish drew out a note case, extracted four five-pound notes from it, also a formal calling card. He wrote on the card with a small, gold pencil. His hand seemed surprisingly steady.

"No. 14 Grinling Crescent," he said. "Have it sent tomorrow without fail. It's . . . it's very heavy. I shall pay the drayage, of course. Mr. Skimp will—" His voice trailed off again. Mr. Skimp wouldn't.

"Oh, that's all right, sir. Mr. Skimp is my uncle."

"Ah, that's too—I mean, well, take this ten-shilling note for yourself, won't you."

Mr. Sutton-Cornish left the shop rather rapidly, his right hand clutching the big key down in his pocket.

An ordinary taxi took him home to dinner. He

dined alone—after three whiskies. But he wasn't as much alone as he looked. He never would be anymore.

It came the next day, swatched in sacking and bound about with cords, looking like nothing on earth.

Four large men in leather aprons perspired it up the four front steps and into the hall, with a good deal of sharp language back and forth. They had a light hoist to help them get it off their dray, but the steps almost beat them. Once inside the hall they got it on two dollies and after that it was just an average heavy, grunting job. They set it up at the back of Mr. Sutton-Cornish's study, across a sort of alcove he had an idea about.

He tipped them liberally, they went away, and Collins, the butler, left the front door open for a while to air the place through.

Carpenters came. The sacking was stripped off, and a framework was built around the door, so that it became part of a partition wall across the alcove. A small door was set in the partition. When the work was done and the mess cleared up, Mr. Sutton-Cornish asked for an oilcan, and locked himself into his study. Then and only then he got out the big bronze key and fitted it again into the huge lock and opened the bronze door wide, both sides of it.

He oiled the hinges from the rear, just in case. Then he shut it again and oiled the lock, removed the key and went for a good long walk, in Kensington Gardens, and back. Collins and the first parlormaid had a look at it while he was out. Cook hadn't been upstairs yet.

"Beats me what the old fool's after," the butler said stonily. "I give him another week, Bruggs. If *she's* not back by then, I give him my notice. How about you, Bruggs?"

"Let him have his fun," Bruggs said, tossing her head. "That old sow he's married to—"

"Bruggs!"

"Tit-tat to you, Mr. Collins," Bruggs said and flounced out of the room.

Mr. Collins remained long enough to sample the whisky in the big square decanter on Mr. Sutton-Cornish's smoking table.

In a shallow, tall cabinet in the alcove behind the bronze door, Mr. Sutton-Cornish arranged a few odds and ends of old china and bric-a-brac and carved ivory and some idols in shiny black wood, very old and unnecessary. It wasn't much of an excuse for so massive a door. He added three statuettes in pink marble. The alcove still had an air of not being quite on to itself. Naturally the bronze door was never open unless the room door was locked.

In the morning Bruggs, or Mary the housemaid, dusted in the alcove, having entered, of course, by the partition door. That amused Mr. Sutton-Cornish slightly, but the amusement began to wear thin. It was about three weeks after his wife and Teddy left that something happened to brighten him up.

A large tawny man with a waxed mustache and

steady gray eyes called on him and presented a card that indicated he was Detective-sergeant Thomas Lloyd of Scotland Yard. He said that one Josiah Skimp, an auctioneer, living in Kennington, was missing from his home to the great concern of his family, and that his nephew, one George William Hawkins, also of Kennington, had happened to mention that Mr. Sutton-Cornish was present in a shop in Soho on the very night when Mr. Skimp vanished. In fact, Mr. Sutton-Cornish might have been the last person known to have spoken to Mr. Skimp.

Mr. Sutton-Cornish laid out the whisky and cigars, placed his fingertips together and nodded gravely.

"I recall him perfectly, Sergeant. In fact I bought that funny door over there from him. Quaint, isn't it?"

The detective glanced at the bronze door, a brief and empty glance.

"Out of my line, sir, I'm afraid. I do recall now something was said about the door. They had quite a job moving it. Very smooth whisky, sir. Very smooth indeed."

"Help yourself, Sergeant. So Mr. Skimp has run off and lost himself. Sorry I can't help you. I really didn't know him, you know."

The detective nodded his large tawny head. "I didn't think you did, sir. The Yard only got the case a couple of days ago. Routine call, you know. Did he seem excited, for instance?"

"He seemed tired," Mr. Sutton-Cornish mused.

"Very fed up—with the whole business of auctioneering, perhaps. I only spoke to him a moment. About that door, you know. A nice little man—but tired."

The detective didn't bother to look at the door again. He finished his whisky and allowed himself a little more.

"No family trouble," he said. "Not much money, but who has these days? No scandal. Not a melancholy type, they say. Odd."

"Some very queer types in Soho," Mr. Sutton-Cornish said mildly.

The detective thought it over. "Harmless, though. A rough district once, but not in our time. Might I ask what you was doing over there?"

"Wandering," Mr. Sutton-Cornish said. "Just wandering. A little more of this?"

"Well, now, really, sir, three whiskies in a morning . . . well, just this once and many thanks to you, sir."

Detective-sergeant Lloyd left—rather regretfully.

After he had been gone ten minutes or so, Mr. Sutton-Cornish got up and locked the study door. He walked softly down the long, narrow room and got the big bronze key out of his inside breast pocket, where he always carried it now.

The door opened noiselessly and easily now. It was well balanced for its weight. He opened it wide, both sides of it.

"Mr. Skimp," he said very gently into the emptiness. "You are wanted by the police, Mr. Skimp."

The fun of that lasted him well on to lunchtime.

In the afternoon Mrs. Sutton-Cornish came back. She appeared quite suddenly before him in the study, sniffed harshly at the smell of tobacco and Scotch, refused a chair and stood very solid and lowering just inside the closed door. Teddy stood beside her for a moment, then hurled himself at the edge of the rug.

"Stop that, you little beast. Stop that at once, darling," Mrs. Sutton-Cornish said. She picked Teddy up and stroked him. He lay in her arms and licked her nose and sneered at Mr. Sutton-Cornish.

"I find," Mrs. Sutton-Cornish said, in a voice that had the brittleness of dry suet, "after numerous very boring interviews with my solicitor, that I can do nothing without your help. Naturally, I dislike asking for that."

Mr. Sutton-Cornish made ineffectual motions towards a chair and when they were ignored he leaned resignedly against the mantelpiece. He said he supposed that was so.

"Perhaps it has escaped your attention that I am still comparatively a young woman. And these are modern days, James."

Mr. Sutton-Cornish smiled wanly and glanced at the bronze door. She hadn't noticed it yet. Then he put his head on one side and wrinkled his nose and said mildly, without much interest:

"You're thinking of a divorce?"

"I'm thinking of very little else," she said brutally.

"And you wish me to compromise myself in the usual manner, at Brighton, with a lady who will be described in court as an actress?"

She glared at him. Teddy helped her glare. Their combined glare failed even to perturb Mr. Sutton-Cornish. He had other resources now.

"Not with that dog," he said carelessly, when she didn't answer.

She made some kind of furious noise, a snort with a touch of snarl in it. She sat down then, very slowly and heavily, a little puzzled. She let Teddy jump to the floor.

"Just what are you talking about, James?" she asked witheringly.

He strolled over to the bronze door, leaned his back against it and explored its rich protuberances with a fingertip. Even then she didn't see the door.

"You want a divorce, my dear Louella," he said slowly, "so that you may marry another man. There's absolutely no point in it—with that dog. I shouldn't be asked to humiliate myself. Too useless. No man would marry that dog."

"James—are you attempting to blackmail me?" Her voice was rather dreadful. She almost bugled. Teddy sneaked across to the window curtains and pretended to lie down.

"And even if he would," Mr. Sutton-Cornish said with a peculiar quiet in his tone, "I oughtn't to make it possible. I ought to have enough human compassion—"

"James! How dare you! You make me physically sick with your insincerity!"

For the first time in his life James Sutton-Cornish laughed in his wife's face.

"Those are two or three of the silliest speeches I ever had to listen to," he said. "You're an elderly, ponderous and damn dull woman. Now run along and take your miserable brown beetle with you."

She got up quickly, very quickly for her, and stood a moment almost swaying. Her eyes were as blank as a blind man's eyes. In the silence Teddy tore fretfully at a curtain, with bitter, preoccupied growls that neither of them noticed.

She said very slowly and almost gently: "We'll see how long you stay in your father's house, James Sutton-Cornish—*pauper*."

She moved very quickly the short distance to the door, went through and slammed it behind her.

The slamming of the door, an unusual event in that household, seemed to awaken a lot of echoes that had not been called upon to perform for a long time. So that Mr. Sutton-Cornish was not instantly aware of the small peculiar sound at his own side of the door, a mixture of sniffing and whimpering, with just a dash of growl.

Teddy. Teddy hadn't made the door. The sudden, bitter exit had for once caught him napping. Teddy was shut in—with Mr. Sutton-Cornish.

For a little while Mr. Sutton-Cornish watched him rather absently, still shaken by the interview, not fully realizing what had happened. The small, wet, black snout explored the crack at the bottom of the closed door. At moments, while the whimpering and sniffing went on, Teddy turned a reddish-brown outjutting eye, like a fat wet marble, towards the man he hated.

Mr. Sutton-Cornish snapped out of it rather suddenly. He straightened and beamed. "Well, well, old man," he purred. "Here we are, and for once without the ladies."

Cunning dawned in his beaming eye. Teddy read it and slipped off under a chair. He was silent now, very silent. And Mr. Sutton-Cornish was silent as he moved swiftly along the wall and turned the key in the study door. Then he sped back towards the alcove, dug the key of the bronze door out of his pocket, unlocked and opened that—wide.

He sauntered back towards Teddy, beyond Teddy, as far as the window.

"Here we are, old man. Jolly, eh? Have a shot of whisky, old man?"

Teddy made a small sound under the chair, and Mr. Sutton-Cornish sidled towards him delicately, bent down suddenly and lunged. Teddy made another chair, farther up the room. He breathed hard and his eyes stuck out rounder and wetter than ever, but he was silent, except for his breathing. And Mr. Sutton-Cornish, stalking him patiently from chair to chair, was as silent as the last leaf of autumn, falling in slow eddies in a windless copse.

At about that time the doorknob turned sharply. Mr. Sutton-Cornish paused to smile and click his tongue. A sharp knock followed. He ignored it. The knocking went on, sharper and sharper, and an angry voice accompanied it.

Mr. Sutton-Cornish went on stalking Teddy.

Teddy did the best he could, but the room was narrow and Mr. Sutton-Cornish was patient and rather agile when he wanted to be. In the interests of agility he was quite willing to be undignified.

The knocking and calling out beyond the door went on, but inside the room things could only end one way. Teddy reached the sill of the bronze door, sniffed at it rapidly, almost lifted a contemptuous hind leg, but didn't because Mr. Sutton-Cornish was too close to him. He sent a low snarl back over his shoulder and hopped that disastrous sill.

Mr. Sutton-Cornish raced back to the room door, turned the key swiftly and silently, crept over to a chair and sprawled in it laughing. He was still laughing when Mrs. Sutton-Cornish thought to try the knob again, found the door yielded this time and stormed into the room. Through the mist of his grisly, solitary laughter he saw her cold stare, then he heard her rustling about the room, heard her calling Teddy.

Then, "What's that thing?" he heard her snap suddenly. "What utter foolishness—Teddy! Come, mother's little lamb! Come, Teddy!"

Even in his laughter Mr. Sutton-Cornish felt the wing of a regret brush his cheek. Poor little Teddy. He stopped laughing and sat up, stiff and alert. The room was too quiet.

"Louella!" he called sharply.

No sound answered him.

He closed his eyes, gulped, opened them again, crept along the room staring. He stood in front of his little alcove for a long time, peering, peering through that bronze portal at the innocent little collection of trivia beyond.

He locked the door with quivering hands, stuffed the key down in his pocket, poured himself a stiff peg of whisky.

A ghostly voice that sounded something like his own, and yet unlike it, said out loud, very close to his ear:

"I didn't really intend anything like that . . . never . . . never—oh, never . . . or . . ."—after a long pause—"did I?"

Braced by the Scotch, he sneaked out into the hall and out of the front door without Collins seeing him. No car waited outside. As luck would have it she had evidently come up from Chinverly by train and taken a taxi. Of course they could trace the taxi—later on, when they tried. A lot of good that would do them.

Collins was next. He thought about Collins for some time, glancing at the bronze door, tempted a good deal, but finally shaking his head negatively.

"Not that way," he muttered. "Have to draw the line somewhere. Can't have a procession—"

He drank some more whisky and rang the bell. Collins made it rather easy for him.

"You rang, sir?"

"What did it sound like?" Mr. Sutton-Cornish asked, a little thick-tongued. "Canaries?"

Collins' chin snapped back a full two inches.

"The dowager won't be here to dinner, Collins.

I think I'll dine out. That's all."

Collins stared at him. A grayness spread over Collins' face, with a little flush at the cheekbones.

"You allude to Mrs. Sutton-Cornish, sir?"

Mr. Sutton-Cornish hiccuped. "Who d'you suppose? Gone back to Chinverly to stew in her own juice some more. Ought to be plenty of it."

With deadly politeness Collins said: "I had meant to ask you, sir, whether Mrs. Sutton-Cornish would return here—permanently. Otherwise—"

"Carry on." Another hiccup.

"Otherwise I should not care to remain myself, sir."

Mr. Sutton-Cornish stood up and went close to Collins and breathed in his face. Haig & Haig. A good breath, of the type.

"Get out!" he rasped. "Get out now! Upstairs with you and pack your things. Your check will be ready for you. A full month. Thirty-two pounds in all, I believe."

Collins stepped back and moved towards the door. "That will suit me perfectly, sir. Thirty-two pounds is the correct amount." He reached the door, spoke again before he opened it. "A reference from *you*, sir, will not be desired."

He went out, closing the door softly.

"Ha!" Mr. Sutton-Cornish said.

Then he grinned slyly, stopped pretending to be angry or drunk and sat down to write the check.

He dined out that night, and the next night, and the next. Cook left on the third day, taking the kitchenmaid with her. That left Bruggs and Mary, the housemaid. On the fifth day Bruggs wept when she gave her notice.

"I'd rather go at once, sir, if you'll let me," she sobbed. "There's something creepy-like about the house since cook and Mr. Collins and Teddy and Mrs. Sutton-Cornish left."

Mr. Sutton-Cornish patted her arm. "Cook and Mr. Collins and Teddy and Mrs. Sutton-Cornish," he repeated. "If only she could hear *that* order of precedence."

Bruggs stared at him, red-eyed. He patted her arm again. "Quite all right, Bruggs. I'll give you your month. And tell Mary to go, too. Think I'll close the house up and live in the south of France for a while. Now, don't cry, Bruggs."

"No, sir." She bawled her way out of the room.

He didn't go to the south of France, of course. Too much fun being right where he was—alone at last in the home of his fathers. Not quite what they would have approved of, perhaps, except possibly the general. But the best he could do.

Almost overnight the house began to have the murmurs of an empty place. He kept the windows closed and the shades down. That seemed to be a gesture of respect he could hardly afford to omit.

Scotland Yard moves with the deadly dependability of a glacier, and at times almost as slowly. So it was a full month and nine days before Detective-sergeant Lloyd came back to No. 14 Grinling Crescent.

By that time the front steps had long since lost their white serenity. The apple-green door had acquired a sinister shade of gray. The brass saucer around the bell, the knocker, the big latch, all these were tarnished and stained, like the brass work of an old freighter limping around the Horn. Those who rang the bell departed slowly, with backward glances, and Mr. Sutton-Cornish would be peeping out at them from the side of a drawn window shade.

He concocted himself weird meals in the echoing kitchen, creeping in after dark with ragged-looking parcels of food. Later he would slink out again with his hat pulled low and his overcoat collar up, give a quick glance up and down the street, then scramble off around the corner. The police constable on duty saw him occasionally at these maneuvers and rubbed his chin a good deal over the situation.

No longer a study even in withered elegance, Mr. Sutton-Cornish became a customer in obscure eating houses where draymen blew their soup on naked tables in compartments like horse stalls; in foreign cafés where men with blue-black hair and pointed shoes dined interminably over minute bottles of wine; in crowded, anonymous tea shops where the food looked and tasted as tired as the people who ate it.

He was no longer a perfectly sane man. In his dry, solitary, poisoned laughter there was the sound of crumbling walls. Even the pinched loafers under the arches of the Thames Embankment, who listened to him because he had sixpences, even these were glad when he passed on, stepping carefully in unshined shoes and lightly swinging the stick he no longer carried.

Then, late one night, returning softly, out of the dull-gray darkness, he found the man from Scotland Yard lurking near the dirty front steps with an air of thinking himself hidden behind a lamp-post.

"I'd like a few words with you, sir," he said, stepping forth briskly and holding his hands as though he might have to use them suddenly.

"Charmed, I'm sure," Mr. Sutton-Cornish chuckled. "Trot right in."

He opened the door with his latchkey, switched the light on and stepped with accustomed ease over a pile of dusty letters on the floor.

"Got rid of the servants," he explained to the detective. "Always did want to be alone someday."

The carpet was covered with burned matches, pipe ash, torn paper, and the corners of the hall had cobwebs in them. Mr. Sutton-Cornish opened his study door, switched the light on in there and stood aside. The detective passed him warily, staring hard at the condition of the house.

Mr. Sutton-Cornish pushed him into a dusty chair, thrust a cigar at him, reached for the whisky decanter.

"Business or pleasure this time?" he inquired archly.

Detective-sergeant Lloyd held his hard hat on his knee and looked the cigar over dubiously. "Smoke it later, thank you, sir. . . . Business, I take it. I'm instructed to make inquiries as to the whereabouts of Mrs. Sutton-Cornish."

Mr. Sutton-Cornish sipped whisky amiably and pointed at the decanter. He took his whisky straight now. "Haven't the least idea," he said. "Why? Down at Chinverly, I suppose. Country place. She owns it."

"It so 'appens she ain't," Detective-sergeant Lloyd said, slipping on an "h"—which he seldom did anymore. "Been a separation, I'm told," he added grimly.

"That's *our* business, old man."

"Up to a point, yes, sir. Granted. Not after her solicitor can't find her and she ain't anywhere anybody can find her. Not *then*, it ain't just your business."

Mr. Sutton-Cornish thought it over. "You might have something there—as the Americans say," he conceded.

The detective passed a large pale hand across his forehead and leaned forward.

"Let's 'ave it, sir," he said quickly. "Best in the long run. Best for all. Nothing to gain by foolishness. The law's the law."

"Have some whisky," Mr. Sutton-Cornish said.

"Not tonight, I won't," Detective-sergeant Lloyd said grimly.

"She left me." Mr. Sutton-Cornish shrugged. "And because of that the servants left me. You know what servants are nowadays. Beyond that I haven't an idea."

"Oh, yus, I think you 'ave," the detective said,

losing a little more of his West End manner. "No charges have been preferred, but I think you know all right, all right."

Mr. Sutton-Cornish smiled airily. The detective scowled and went on: "We've taken the liberty of watching you, and for a gentleman of your position—you've been living a damn queer life, if I may say so."

"You may say so, and then you may get to hell out of my house," Mr. Sutton-Cornish said suddenly.

"Not so fast. Not yet I won't."

"Perhaps you would like to search the house."

"Per'aps I should. Per'aps I shall. No hurry there. Takes time. Sometimes takes shovels." Detective-sergeant Lloyd permitted himself to leer rather nastily. "Seems to me like people does a bit of disappearin' when you 'appen to be around. Take that Skimp. Now take Mrs. Sutton-Cornish."

Mr. Sutton-Cornish stared at him with lingering malice. "And in your experience, Sergeant, where do people go when they disappear?"

"Sometimes they don't disappear. Sometimes somebody disappears them." The detective licked his strong lips, with a catlike expression.

Mr. Sutton-Cornish slowly raised his arm and pointed to the bronze door. "You wanted it, Sergeant," he said suavely. "You shall have it. There is where you should look for Mr. Skimp, for Teddy the Pomeranian and for my wife. There—behind that ancient door of bronze."

The detective didn't shift his gaze. For a long

moment he didn't change expression. Then, quite amiably, he grinned. There was something else behind his eyes, but it was behind them.

"Let's you and me take a nice little walk," he said breezily. "The fresh air would do you a lot of good, sir. Let's—"

"There," Mr. Sutton-Cornish announced, still pointing with his arm rigid, "behind that door."

"Ah-ah." Detective-sergeant Lloyd waggled a large finger roguishly. "Been alone too much, you 'ave, sir. Thinkin' about things. Do it myself once in a while. Gets a fellow balmy in the crumpet like. Take a nice little walk with me, sir. We could stop somewhere for a nice—" The big tawny man planted a forefinger on the end of his nose and pushed his head back and wiggled his little finger in the air at the same time. But his steady gray eyes remained in another mood.

"We look at my bronze door first."

Mr. Sutton-Cornish skipped out of his chair. The detective had him by the arm in a flash. "None of that," he said in a frosty voice. "Hold still."

"Key in here," Mr. Sutton-Cornish said, pointing at his breast pocket but not trying to get his hand into it.

The detective got it out for him, stared at it heavily.

"All behind the door—on meathooks," Mr. Sutton-Cornish said. "All three. Little meathook for Teddy. Very large meathook for my wife. *Very* large meathook."

Holding him with his left hand, Detective-sergeant Lloyd thought it over. His pale brows were drawn tight. His large weathered face was grim—but skeptical.

"No harm to look," he said finally.

He marched Mr. Sutton-Cornish across the floor, pushed the bronze key into the huge antique lock, twisted the ring and opened the door.

He opened both sides of it. He stood looking into that very innocent alcove with its cabinets of knick-knacks and absolutely nothing else. He became genial again.

"Meathooks, did you say, sir? Very cute, if I may say so."

He laughed, released Mr. Sutton-Cornish's arm and teetered on his heels.

"What the hell's it for?" he asked.

Mr. Sutton-Cornish doubled over very swiftly and launched his thin body with furious speed at the big detective.

"Take a little walk yourself—and find out!" he screamed.

Detective-sergeant Lloyd was a big and solid man and probably used to being butted. Mr. Sutton-Cornish could hardly have moved him six inches, even with a running start. But the bronze door had a high sill. The detective moved with the deceptive quickness of his trade, swayed his body just enough and jarred his foot against the bronze sill.

If it hadn't been for that, he would have plucked Mr. Sutton-Cornish neatly out of the air and held him squirming like a kitten, between his large thumb and forefinger. But the sill jarred him off balance.

He stumbled a little, and swayed his body completely out of Mr. Sutton-Cornish's way.

Mr. Sutton-Cornish butted empty space—the empty space framed by that majestic door of bronze. He sprawled forward clutching—falling—clutching—across the sill—

Detective-sergeant Lloyd straightened up slowly, twisted his thick neck and stared. He moved back a little from the sill so that he could be perfectly certain the side of the door hid nothing from him. It didn't. He saw a cabinet of odd pieces of china, odds and ends of carved ivory and shiny black wood, and on top of the cabinet three little statuettes of pink marble.

He saw nothing else. There was nothing else in there to see.

"Gorblimey!" he said at last, violently. At least he thought he said it. Somebody said it. He wasn't quite sure. He was never absolutely sure about anything—after that night.

The whisky looked all right. It smelled all right, too. Shaking so that he could hardly hold the decanter, Detective-sergeant Lloyd poured a little into a glass and took a sip in his dry mouth and waited.

After a little while he drank another spoonful. He waited again. Then he drank a stiff drink—a very stiff drink.

He sat down in the chair beside the whisky and took his large folded cotton handkerchief out of his pocket and unfolded it slowly and mopped his face and neck behind his ears.

In a little while he wasn't shaking quite so much.

Warmth began to flow through him. He stood up, drank some more whisky, then slowly and bitterly moved back down the room. He swung the bronze door shut, locked it, put the key down in his pocket. He opened the partition door at the side, braced himself and stepped through into the alcove. He looked at the back of the bronze door. He touched it. It wasn't very light in there, but he could see that the place was empty, except for the silly-looking cabinet. He came out again shaking his head.

"Can't be," he said out loud. "Not a chance. Not 'arf a chance."

Then, with a sudden unreasonableness of the reasonable man, he flew into a rage.

"If I get 'ooked for this," he said between his teeth, "I get 'ooked."

He went down to the dark cellar, rummaged around until he found a hand ax and carried it back upstairs.

He hacked the woodwork to ribbons. When he was done, the bronze door stood alone on its base, jagged wood all around it, but not holding it any longer. Detective-sergeant Lloyd put the hand ax down, wiped his hands and face on his big handkerchief and went on behind the door. He put his shoulder to it and set his strong, yellow teeth.

Only a brutally determined man of immense strength could have done it. The door fell forward with a heavy rumbling crash that seemed to shake the whole house. The echoes of that crash died away slowly, along infinite corridors of unbelief.

Then the house was silent again. The big man went out into the hall and had another look out of the front door.

He put his coat on, adjusted his hard hat, folded his damp handkerchief carefully and put it in his hip pocket, lit the cigar Mr. Sutton-Cornish had given him, took a drink of whisky and swaggered to the door.

At the door he turned and deliberately sneered at the bronze door, lying fallen but still huge in the welter of splintered wood.

"To 'ell with you, 'ooever you are," Detective-sergeant Lloyd said. "I ain't no bloody primrose."

He shut the house door behind him. A little high fog outside, a few dim stars, a quiet street with lighted windows. Two or three cars of expensive appearance, very likely chauffeurs lounging in them, but no one in sight.

He crossed the street at an angle and walked along beside the tall iron railing of the park. Faintly through the rhododendron bushes he could see the dull glimmer of the little ornamental lake. He looked up and down the street and took the big bronze key out of his pocket.

"Make it a good 'un," he told himself softly.

His arm swept up and over. There was a minute splash in the ornamental lake, then silence. Detective-sergeant Lloyd walked on calmly, puffing at his cigar.

Back at C.I.D. he gave his report steadily, and for the first and last time in his life, there was something besides truth in it. Couldn't raise anybody at the house. All dark. Waited three hours. Must all be away.

The inspector nodded and yawned.

The Sutton-Cornish heirs eventually pried the estate out of Chancery and opened up No. 14 Grinling Crescent and found the bronze door lying in a welter of dust and splintered wood and matted cobwebs. They stared at it goggle-eyed, and when they found out what it was, sent for dealers, thinking there might be a little money in it. But the dealers sighed and said no, no money in that sort of thing now. Better ship it off to a foundry and have it melted down for the metal. Get so much a pound. The dealers departed noiselessly with wry smiles.

Sometimes when things are a little dull in the Missing Persons section of the C.I.D. they take out the Sutton-Cornish file and dust it off and look through it sourly and put it away again.

Sometimes when Inspector—formerly Detective-sergeant—Thomas Lloyd is walking along an unusually dark and quiet street he will whirl suddenly, for no reason at all, and jump to one side with a swift anguished agility.

But there isn't really anybody there, trying to butt him.

Slip Stream

Sheila Hodgson

He had not liked the job. He was a man in his late forties, a charter pilot accustomed to strain and indifferent to people. Half the shares in the company belonged to him; he was a director of Sonic Flights. He worked long hours in his own interest and took whatever came in the name of profit.

He did not like the job.

It was perhaps the time of year, misty December running up to Christmas. It could have been the passengers, a noisy mob on their way to a jazz festival in the Channel Islands. Captain Armitage disliked pop and ignored the swinging scene; he saw to it that the tour manager paid heavily in advance. He got his clearance from ground control and the aircraft swung lazily into the gray autumnal sky.

They were over the Channel when the fog dropped

down, lapping round them in thick billows. Armitage swore. He was not afraid of the calculated risk; but he knew that a quick turnaround, a rigid time schedule, made all the difference between profit and loss. Captain Armitage was on a percentage and had no intention of showing a loss.

"Ladies and gentlemen. This is your captain speaking." It always paid to make soothing noises at the customers. "Owing to adverse weather conditions we shall be approximately ten minutes late in arriving. Sonic Flights apologizes for any inconvenience." The loudspeaker crackled regretfully and fell silent.

"Late?" said the copilot, and he was a young man with bleak eyes. "You're not going to try and land in this?"

Armitage grunted. He disliked Chris David, a grammar-school type who knew too much technology and not enough about the guts of flying. A creep who flew by mathematics. Armitage flew on a wing and a prayer, and had once been arrested for piloting his Tiger Moth under the Tower Bridge for a bet.

"We have a bad report."

He would never have employed Chris David but staff were hard to get at the money he was prepared to pay.

The fog curdled, clots of acid vapor clinging to the tail. They seemed to be the last thing left alive.

"Don't want to disappoint the kids," said Captain Armitage heartily. The aircraft shook and muttered; it seemed to hang without movement amongst the yellowing cloud. The air parted and lightened and then darkened and closed in on them again. Three thousand feet below the islands spoke. The voice sliced upwards through the fog and ordered the pilot to return to England.

"Ladies and gentlemen. This is your captain speaking." The loudspeaker gave no hint of Armitage's sour anger. "I am sorry to tell you that weather conditions make it impossible to land. We are therefore flying back to base. Another attempt will be made later in the day."

"Next time I'll walk," said one of the passengers. Jeering applause greeted the remark, a laugh ran through the cabin. Somebody began to play softly on the mouth organ—go, tell it on a mountain—somebody else handed a bottle of Coke across the aisle. They were not concerned. It was a drag, a bind: soon the mechanical age for which they had such contempt would put everything right and put them down where they wanted to be.

Over the coast the fog thinned to a dirty mist; by the time they approached the airfield the visibility was fair to good. The controller okayed him to land, Armitage swept down the glide path—and stared.

Parked straight across the runway was a light aircraft.

He swore. He jerked the nose up; he lifted sharply and circled the gray sky. Armitage had seen some crazy things in the past, had done five or six himself—but this was not funny, this was going to lead to a full inquiry, thank you very much. He felt himself shaking. It was a full minute before he even heard the controller's voice.

"Ariel five seven, why are you overshooting?"

Armitage replied with some violence. Beside him he could hear Chris David gasp, and no wonder.

"Did you see that—?" cried Armitage. "Did you see that? Ground control must be drunk or crazy. What the hell are they playing at down there?" He repeated the question savagely into the mike. There was a crackling silence, and then:

"Ariel five seven, why are you overshooting?" The voice sounded puzzled; no more.

It occurred to Armitage that his sight was playing tricks. He was forty-eight and had never felt better; but he treated his body as he did the machine, pushing his demands to the limit. He was forty-eight, the eyeball changed; he made a mental note to go to the oculist after Christmas. He gave instructions to switch over to the instrument-landing system and approach the glide path a second time. As they dropped through the clouds the runway rose smoothly in front of them: and there it was again.

A light aircraft slap across their route.

Armitage yelled. He swung the machine up and away; he exploded into a torrent of blasphemy. The control tower cried harshly from below.

"Ariel five seven, Ariel five seven! Do you read? Why are you overshooting, Ariel five seven?"

He became aware of Chris David's flat astonished eyes.

"We're diverting to Keston."

"Why?"

"Because," said Armitage grimly, "whatever is going on down there, I want no part of it." He ignored the copilot's protests. The man was a fool. Incompetent. Dangerous. The engines droned and the cabin shuddered and another sound split the thin air. After a while—

"For pity's sake!" And it was too much, it was too bad. "Who's playing music?"

"What?"

"I've got enough on my plate. Tell those blasted clowns back there to shut up."

"Nobody's playing music."

Yet he could hear it. A rhythmic jazz beat, now loud, now soft. Fear sucked at his throat: he was overworked, he was under pressure.

"When we get to Keston," said Armitage in a tight voice, "you'd better bring her down."

The control tower at Keston was clearly expecting them, had obviously been warned. The controller sounded tense and authoritative; there was no fog here. At less than a thousand feet David gasped, seized the controls—and flung the aircraft skywards.

"What did you see?" asked Armitage. But he knew the answer.

They flew on to three more airfields; and at each the pattern was the same. Unrest began to spread through the cabin; David went back to quieten the passengers, reassure them. It was not easy. It was not easy to explain that they were not landing because he and the captain saw—thought they saw—

On his way to the flight deck a kind of syncopated throbbing shook the air, the wail of some jazz instrument. He glanced over his shoulder. All the passengers were strapped in.

"About that music," said Chris David.

Armitage nodded.

They began to analyze it obsessively, drawn together by the unnatural fellowship of fear. After the last attempt at landing Armitage exclaimed—

"It's the same aircraft! You realize that?"

David looked at him.

"Whatever airfield we try, we're blocked by the same aircraft! Which is not possible."

"Hallucination?"

"And I'll tell you something else, boy. I'll tell you." Armitage loosened his collar. It was very hot. "That—that thing down there dates from the Second World War. It's obsolete. It's American, too."

"We are," said Chris David carefully, "having some kind of hallucination." He gave a dry cough.

"Do you want to gamble on it?"

"What?"

"Do you want to gamble on its not really being there?"

"We can't do that!"

"Thank you." Armitage dried his hands; sweat was trickling down the palms. "All the same, we've got to do something, and pretty damn fast. Or we shall run out of fuel."

The clouds puffed by and the sky yawned above them.

Down below a full-scale alert had been sounded.

Four airfields reported the incident; organization tensed to meet a crisis. The flight had been checked, the passengers identified, and the fact that they were on their way to a jazz festival noted. The official view was that both pilot and passengers were under the influence of drugs. High above, Armitage cruised on through space. When his fears became actual he came to a decision and spoke to Chris David and crash-landed in the English Channel.

They were picked up within the hour, unhurt, already the object of a massive search. In the confusion of relief they lost touch; for one brief moment David saw his pilot standing on the deck. His eyes were fixed on the sky, the head tilted like a man who strains to catch a fading voice.

"All right?" cried David.

Captain Armitage nodded. He tried to hum, but the music eluded him; he tried to remember, but the tune had gone.

It was weeks later when both men were summoned to appear before an investigatory committee. There was a report in from the salvage party, and the chairman held it up.

"You gentlemen were luckier than you knew." He tossed the report on the table. "There was a serious fault in your undercarriage."

"Oh?"

"It is not," said the chairman, "the purpose of my committee to pass judgment on your maintenance. But I have to tell you this. If you had come down on dry land you would, in the opinion of our experts, have blown yourselves to glory."

It was, as agreed on leaving the building, coincidence, Luck. Fate. The long arm of chance. Whatever delusion had prevented them from landing—

"Instinct." Captain Armitage unrolled his umbrella; it was beginning to rain. "A trained pilot develops a kind of extra sense, a nose for danger. He can tell."

"I don't know." Chris David frowned. "I did a bit of research—out of curiosity. You see, I remembered the name of the tune—"

"What tune?"

"The tune we both heard!"

"I didn't hear any tune," said Armitage, and genuinely believed it.

Chris David clutched his arm. "There was an American musician who disappeared over the Channel. During the war. It was Christmas then, and he was on his way to a concert in Paris. You know the man?"

"No," said Captain Armitage, and hailed a taxi. He did not believe in ghosts and he was not interested in jazz musicians.

The Quest for "Blank Claveringi"

Patricia Highsmith

Avery Clavering, a professor of zoology at a California university, heard of the giant snails of Kuwa in a footnote of a book on mollusks. His sabbatical had been coming up in three months when he read the few lines:

> It is said by Matusas Islands natives that snails even larger than this exist on the uninhabited island of Kuwa, twenty-five miles distant from the Matusas. The Matusans claim that these snails have a shell diameter of twenty feet and that they are man-eating. Professor Wm. J. Stead, now living in the Matusas, visited Kuwa in 1949 without finding any snails at all, but the legend persists.

The item aroused Professor Clavering's interest, because he very much wanted to discover some animal, bird, reptile or even mollusk to which he

could give his name. *Something-or-other Claveringi.*
The professor was forty-eight. His time, perhaps,
was not growing short, but he had achieved no
particular renown. The discovery of a new species
would win him immortality in his field.

The Matusas, the professor saw on a map, were
three small islands arranged like the points of an
isosceles triangle not far from Hawaii. He wrote a
letter to Dr. Stead and received the following reply,
written on an abominable typewriter, so many words
pale, he could scarcely read it:

April 8th, 19—

Dear Professor Clavering:

I have long heard of the giant snails of Kuwa,
but before you make a trip of such length, I must
tell you that the natives here assure me a group of
them went about twenty years ago to Kuwa to ex-
terminate these so-called man-eating snails which
they imagined could swim the ocean between Kuwa
and the Matusas and do some damage to the latter
islands. They claim to have killed off the whole
community of them except for one old fellow they
could not kill. This is typical of native stories—
there's always one that got away. I haven't much
doubt the snails were no bigger than three feet
across and that they were not **** [here a word was
illegible, due both to the pale ribbon and a squashed
insect]. You say you read of my effort in 1949 to
find the giant snails. What the footnote did not say
is that I have made several trips since to find them.
I retired to the Matusas, in fact, for that purpose.
I now believe the snails to be mere folklore, a fig-

ment of the natives' imagination. If I were you, I would not waste time or money on an expedition.

Yours sincerely,
Prof. Wm. J. Stead

Professor Clavering had the money and the time. He detected a sourness in Dr. Stead's letter. Maybe Dr. Stead had just had bad luck. By post, Professor Clavering hired a thirty-foot sailboat with an auxiliary motor from Hawaii. He wanted to make the trip alone from the Matusas. *Blank Claveringi*. Regardless of the size, the snail was apt to be different from any known snail, because of its isolation—if it existed.

He planned to go one month ahead of his wife and to join her and their twenty-year-old daughter, Wanda, in Hawaii for a more orthodox holiday after he had visited Kuwa. A month would give him plenty of time to find the snail, even if there were only one, to take photographs and make notes.

It was late June when Professor Clavering, equipped with water tanks, tinned beef, soup and milk, biscuits, writing materials, camera, knife, hatchet and a Winchester .22 which he hardly knew how to use, set forth from one of the Matusas bound for Kuwa. Dr. Stead, who had been his host for a few days, saw him off. Dr. Stead was seventy-five, he said, but he looked older, due perhaps to the ravages of drink and the apparently aimless life he led now. He had not looked for the giant snail in two years, he said.

"I've given the last third of my life to looking for this snail, you might say," Dr. Stead added. "But that's man's fate, I suppose, the pursuit of the non-existent. Well—good luck to you, Professor Clavering!" He waved his old American straw hat as the *Samantha* left the dock under motor power.

Professor Clavering had made out with Dr. Stead that if he did find snails, he would come back at once, get some natives to accompany him and return to Kuwa with materials to make crates for the snails. Dr. Stead had expressed doubt whether he would persuade any natives to accompany him, if the snail or snails were really large. But then, Dr. Stead had been negative about everything pertaining to Professor Clavering's quest. Professor Clavering was glad to get away from him.

After about an hour, Professor Clavering cut the motor and tentatively hoisted some sail. The wind was favorable, but he knew little about sails, and he paid close attention to his compass. At last, Kuwa came into view, a tan hump on a sea of blue. He was quite close before he saw any greenery, and this was only the tops of some trees. Already, he was looking for anything resembling a giant snail, and regretting he had not brought binoculars, but the island was only three miles long and one mile broad. He decided to aim for a small beach. He dropped anchor, two of them, in water so clear, he could see the sand under it. He stood for a few minutes on the deck.

The only life he saw was a few birds in the tops of trees, brightly colored, crested birds, making cries he had never heard before. There was no low-lying vegetation whatsoever, none of the grass and reeds that might have been expected on an island such as this—much like the Matusas in soil color—and this augured well of the presence of snails that might have devoured everything green within their reach.

It was only a quarter to two. Professor Clavering ate part of a papaya, two boiled eggs, and brewed coffee on his alcohol burner, as he had had nothing to eat since 6 a.m. Then with his hunting knife and hatchet in the belt of his khaki shorts, and his camera around his neck, he lowered himself into the water. The *Samantha* carried no rowboat.

He sank up to his neck, but he could walk on the bottom. He held the camera high. He emerged panting, as he was some twenty pounds over-weight. Professor Clavering was to regret every one of those pounds before the day was over, but as he got his breath and looked around him, and felt himself drying off in the warm sunlight, he was happy. He wiped his hatchet and knife with dry sand, then walked inland, alert for the rounded form of a snail's shell, moving or stationary, any-where. But as snails were more or less nocturnal, he thought any snails might well be sleeping in some cave or crevice with no idea of emerging until nightfall.

He decided to cross the island first, then follow the coast to right or left and circle the island. He had not gone a quarter of a mile, when his heart gave a leap. Ten yards before him, he saw three bent saplings with their top leaves chewed off. The young trees were four inches in diameter at their bases. It would have taken a considerable weight to bend them down, something like a hundred pounds. The professor looked on the trees and the ground for the glaze left by snails, but found none. But rain could have washed it away. A snail whose shell was three feet in diameter would not weigh enough to bend such a tree, so Professor Clavering now hoped for something bigger. He pushed on.

He arrived at the other side of the island. The sea had eaten a notch into the shore, forming a mostly dry gully of a hundred yards' length and a depth of thirty feet. The land here was sandy but moist, and there was, he saw, a little vegetation in the form of patchy grass. But here, the lower branches of all the trees had been divested of their leaves, and so long ago that the branches had dried and fallen off. All this bespoke the presence of land snails.

Professor Clavering stooped and looked down into the gully. He saw, just over the edge of his side of the crevice, the pink-tan curve of something that was neither rock nor sand. If it was a snail, it was monstrous. Involuntarily, he took a step backward, scattering pebbles down the gully.

The professor ran round the gully to have a better look. It was a snail, and its shell was about fifteen feet high. He had a view of its left side, the side without the spiral. It resembled a peach-colored sail filled with wind, and the sunlight made nacreous, silvery patches gleam and twinkle as the great thing stirred. The little rain of pebbles had aroused it, the professor realized. If the shell was fifteen or eighteen feet in diameter, he reckoned that the snail's body or foot would be something like six yards long when extended.

Rooted to the spot, the professor stood, thrilled as much by the (as yet) empty phrase *Blank Claveringi* which throbbed in his head as by the fact he was looking upon something no man had before, or at least no scientist. The crate would have to be bigger than he had thought, but the *Samantha* would be capable of taking it on her forward deck.

The snail was backing to pull its head from the narrow part of the gully. The moist body, the color of tea with milk, came into view with the slowness of an enormous snake awakening from slumber. All was silent, except for pebbles dropping from the snail's underside as it lifted its head, except for the professor's constrained breathing. The snail's head, facing inland, rose higher and higher, and its antennae, with which it saw, began to extend. Professor Clavering realized he had disturbed it from its diurnal sleep, and a brief terror caused him to retreat again, sending more pebbles down the slope.

The snail heard this, and slowly turned its enormous head toward him.

The professor felt paralyzed. A gigantic face regarded him, a face with drooping, scalloped cheeks or lips, with antennae six feet long now, the eyes on the end of them scrutinizing him at his own level and scarcely ten feet away, with the disdain of a Herculean lorgnette, with the unknown potency of a pair of oversized telescopes. The snail reared so high, it had to arch its antennae to keep him in view. Six yards long? It would be more like eight or ten yards. The snail turned itself to move toward him.

Still, the professor did not budge. He knew about snails' teeth, the twenty-odd thousand pairs of them even in a small garden snail, set in comblike structures, the upper front teeth visible, moving up and down constantly just under transparent flesh. A snail of this size, with proportionate teeth, could chew through a tree as quickly as a woodsman's ax, the professor thought.

The snail was advancing up the bank with monumental confidence. He had to stand still for a few seconds simply to admire it. *His* snail! The professor opened his camera and took a picture, just as the snail was hauling its shell over the edge of the gully.

"You are magnificent!" Professor Clavering said in a soft and awe-struck voice. Then he took a few steps backward.

It was pleasant to think he could skip nimbly about, comparatively speaking, observing the snail from all angles, while the snail could only creep toward him at what seemed the rate of one yard in ten seconds. The professor thought to watch the snail for an hour or so, then go back to the *Samantha* and write some notes. He would sleep aboard the boat, take some more photographs tomorrow morning, then start under engine power back to the Matusas. He trotted for twenty yards, then turned to watch the snail approach.

The snail traveled with its head lifted three feet above the ground, keeping the professor in the focus of its eyes. It was moving faster. Professor Clavering retreated sooner than he intended, and before he could get another picture.

Now Professor Clavering looked around for a mate of the snail. He was rather glad not to see another snail, but he cautioned himself not to rule out the possibility of a mate. It wouldn't be pleasant to be cornered by two snails, yet the idea excited him. Impossible to think of a situation in which he could not escape from two slow, lumbering creatures like the—the what? *Amygdalus Persica* (his mind stuck on peaches, because of the beautiful color of the shell) *Carnivora* (perhaps) *Claveringi*. That could be improved upon, the professor thought as he walked backward, watching.

A little grove of trees gave him an idea. If he stood in the grove, the snail could not reach him, and he would also have a close view. The professor took a stand amid twelve or fifteen trees, all about twenty feet high. The snail did not slacken its speed, but began to circle the grove, still watching the professor. Finding no opening big enough between two trees, the snail raised its head higher, fifteen feet high, and began to creep up on the trees. Branches cracked, and one tree snapped.

Professor Clavering ducked and retreated. He had a glimpse of a great belly gliding unhurt over a jagged tree trunk, of a circular mouth two feet across, open and showing the still wider upper band of teeth like sharks' teeth, munching automatically up and down. The snail cruised gently down over the treetops, some of which sprang back into position as the snail's weight left them.

Click! went the professor's camera.

What a sight that had been! Something like a slow hurdle. He imagined entertaining friends with an account of it, substantiated by the photograph, once he got back to California. Old Professor McIlroy of the biology department had laughed at him for spending seven thousand dollars on an effort he predicted would be futile!

Professor Clavering was tiring, so he cut directly for the *Samantha*. He noticed that the snail veered also in a direction that would intercept him, if they kept on at their steady though different speeds, and the professor chuckled and trotted for a bit. The snail also picked up speed, and the professor remembered the wide, upward rippling of the snail's body as it had hurdled the trees. It would be interesting to see how fast the snail could go on a straightaway course. Such a test would have to wait for America.

He reached the water and saw his beach a few yards away to his right, but no ship was there. He'd made a mistake, he thought, and his beach was on the other side of the island. Then he caught sight of the *Samantha* half a mile out on the ocean, drifting away.

"*Damn!*" Professor Clavering said aloud. He'd done something wrong with the anchors. Did he dare try to swim to it? The distance frightened him, and it was growing wider every moment.

A rattle of pebbles behind him made him turn. The snail was hardly twenty feet away.

The professor trotted down toward the beach. There was bound to be some slit on the coast, a cave however small, where he could be out of reach of the snail. He wanted to rest for a while. What really annoyed him now was the prospect of a chilly night without blankets or food. The Matusas natives had been right: there was nothing to eat on Kuwa.

Professor Clavering stopped dead, his shoes sliding on sand and pebbles. Before him, not fifty feet away on the beach, was another snail as big as the one following him, and somewhat lighter in color. Its tail was in the sea, and its muzzle dripped water as it reared itself to get a look at him.

It was this snail, the professor realized, that had chewed through the hemp ropes and let the boat go free. Was there something about new hemp ropes that appealed to snails? This question he put out of his mind for the nonce. He had a snail before and behind him. The professor trotted on along the shore. The only crevice of shelter he was sure existed was the niche on the other side of the island. He forced himself to walk at a moderate pace for a while, to breathe normally, then he sat down and treated himself to a rest.

The first snail was the first to appear, and as it had lost sight of him, it lifted its head and looked slowly to right and left, though without slacking its progress. The professor sat motionless, bare head lowered, hoping the snail would not see him. But he was not that lucky. The snail saw him and altered its course to a straight line for him. Behind it came the second snail—its wife? its husband? The professor could not tell and there was no way of telling.

Professor Clavering had to leave his resting place. The weight of his hatchet reminded him that he at least had a weapon. A good scare, he thought, a minor wound might discourage them. He knew they were hungry, that their teeth could tear his flesh more easily than they tore trees, and that alive or dead, he would be eaten by these snails if he permitted it to happen. He drew his hatchet and faced them, conscious that he cut a not very formidable figure with his slight paunch, his pale, skinny legs, his height of five feet seven, about a third the snails' height, but his brows above his glasses were set with a determination to defend his life.

The first snail reared when it was ten feet away. The professor advanced and swung the hatchet at the projecting mantle on the snail's left side. He had not dared get close enough, his aim was inches short, and the weight of the hatchet pulled the professor off balance. He staggered and fell under the raised muzzle, and had just time to roll himself from under the descending mouth before it touched the ground where he had been.

Angry now, he circled the snail and swung a blow at the nacreous shell, which turned the blade. The hatchet took an inch-deep chip, but nothing more. The professor swung again, higher this time and in the center of the shell's posterior, trying for the lung valve beneath, but the valve was still higher, he knew, ten feet from the ground, and once more his hatchet took only a chip. The snail began to turn itself to face him.

The professor then confronted the second snail, rushed at it and swung the hatchet, cutting it in the cheek. The hatchet sank up to its wooden handle, and he had to tug to get it out, and then had to run a few yards, as the snail put on speed and reared its head for a biting attack. Glancing back, the professor saw that no liquid (he had not, of course, expected blood) came from the cut in the snail's cheek, and in fact he couldn't see the cut. And the blow had certainly been no discouragement to the snail's advance.

Professor Clavering began to walk at a sensible pace straight for the snails' lair on the other side of the island. By the time he scrambled down the side of the gully, he was winded and his legs hurt. But he saw to his relief that the gorge narrowed to a sharp V. Wedged in that, he would be safe. Professor Clavering started into the V, which had an overhanging top rather like a cave, when he saw that what he had taken for some rounded rocks were moving—at least some of them were. They were baby snails! They were larger than good-sized beach balls. And the professor saw, from the way a couple of them were devouring grass blades, that they were hungry.

A snail's head appeared high on his left. The giant parent snail began to descend the gully. A crepitation, a pair of antennae against the sky on his right, heralded the arrival of the second snail. He had nowhere to turn except the sea, which was not a bad idea, he thought, as these were land snails. The professor waded out and turned left, walking waist-deep in water. It was slow going, and a snail was coming after him. He got closer to the land and ran in thigh-deep water.

The first snail, the darker one, entered the water boldly and crept along in a depth of several inches, showing signs of being willing to go into deeper water when it got abreast of Professor Clavering. The professor hoped the other snail, maybe the mother, had stayed with the young. But it hadn't. It was following along the land, and accelerating. The professor plunged wildly for the shore where he would be able to move faster.

Now, thank goodness, he saw rocks. Great igneous masses of rocks covered a sloping hill down to the sea. There was bound to be a niche, some place there where he could take shelter. The sun was sinking into the ocean, it would be dark soon, and there was no moon, he knew. The professor was thirsty. When he reached the rocks, he flung himself like a corpse into a trough made by four or five scratchy boulders, which caused him to lie in a curve. The rocks rose two feet above his body, and the trough was hardly a foot wide. A snail couldn't, he reasoned, stick its head down here and bite him.

The peachy curves of the snails' shells appeared, and one, the second, drew closer.

"I'll strike it with my hatchet if it comes!" the professor swore to himself. "I'll cut its face to ribbons with my knife!" He was now reconciled to killing both adults, because he could take back a pair of the young ones, and in fact more easily because they were smaller.

The snail seemed to sniff like a dog, though inaudibly, as its muzzle hovered over the professor's hiding place. Then the snail with majestic calm came down on the rocks between which the professor lay. Its slimy foot covered the aperture and within seconds had blocked out almost all the light.

Professor Clavering drew his hunting knife in anger and panic, and plunged it several times into the snail's soft flesh. The snail seemed not even to wince. A few seconds later, it stopped moving, though the professor knew that it was not only not dead, as the stabs hadn't touched any vital organs, but that it had fastened itself over his trench in the firmest possible way. No slit of light showed. The professor was only grateful that the irregularity of the rocks must afford a supply of air.

Now he pressed frantically with his palms against the snail's body, and felt his hand slip and scrape against rock. The firmness of the snail, his inability to budge it, made him feel slightly sick for a moment.

An hour passed. The professor almost slept, but the experience was more like a prolonged hallucination. He dreamed, or feared, that he was being chewed by twenty thousand pairs of teeth into a heap of ground meat, which the two giant snails shared with their offspring. To add to his misery, he was cold and hungry. The snail's body gave no warmth, and was even cool.

Some hours later, the professor awoke and saw stars above him. The snail had departed. It was pitch dark. He stood up cautiously, trying not to make a sound, and stepped out of the crevice. He was free! On a sandy stretch of beach a few yards away, Professor Clavering lay down, pressed against a vertical face of rock. Here he slept the remaining hours until dawn.

He awakened just in time, and perhaps not the dawn but a sixth sense had awakened him. The first snail was coming toward him and was only ten feet away. The professor got up on trembling legs, and trotted inland, up a slope. An idea came to him: if he could push a boulder of, say, five hundred pounds—possible with a lever—onto an adult snail in the gully, and smash the spot below which its lung lay, then he could kill it. Otherwise, he could think of no other means at his disposal that could inflict a fatal injury. His gun might, but the gun was on the *Samantha*.

He had already estimated that it might be a week, or never, that help would come from the Matusas. The *Samantha* would not necessarily float back to the Matusas, would not necessarily be seen by any other ship for days, and even if it was seen, would it be apparent she was drifting? And if so, would the spotters make a beeline for the Matusas to report it? Not necessarily.

The professor bent quickly and licked some dew

from a leaf. The snails were twenty yards behind him now.

The trouble is, I'm becoming exhausted, he said to himself.

He was even more tired at noon. Only one snail pursued him, but the professor imagined the other resting or eating a treetop, in order to be fresh later. The professor could trot a hundred yards, find a spot to rest in, but he dared not shut his eyes for long, lest he sleep. And he was definitely weak from lack of food.

So the day passed. His idea of dropping a rock down the gully was thwarted by two factors: the second snail was guarding the gully now, at the top of its V, and there was no such rock as he needed within a hundred yards.

When dusk came, the professor could not find the hill where the igneous rocks were. Both snails had him in their sight now. His watch said a quarter to seven.

Professor Clavering took a deep breath and faced the fact that he must make an attempt to kill one or both snails before dark. Almost without thinking, or planning—he was too spent for that—he chopped down a slender tree and hacked off its branches. The leaves of these branches were devoured by the two snails five minutes after the branches had fallen to the ground. The professor dragged his tree several yards inland, and sharpened one end of it with the hatchet. It was too heavy a weapon for one hand to wield, but in two hands, it made a kind of battering ram, or giant spear.

At once, Professor Clavering turned and attacked, running with the spear pointed slightly upward. He aimed for the first snail's mouth, but struck too low, and the tree end penetrated about four inches into the snail's chest—or the area below its face. No vital organ here, except the long, straight esophagus, which in these giant snails would be set deeper than four inches. He had nothing for his trouble but lacerated hands. His spear hung for a few seconds in the snail's flesh, then fell out onto the ground. The professor retreated, pulling his hatchet from his belt.

The second snail, coming up abreast of the other, paused to chew off a few inches of the tree stump, then joined its mate in giving attention to Professor Clavering. There was something contemptuous, something absolutely assured, about the snails' slow progress toward him, as if they were thinking, "Escape us a hundred, a thousand times, we shall finally reach you and devour every trace of you."

The professor advanced once more, circled the snail he had just hit with the tree spear and swung his hatchet at the rear of its shell. Desperately, he attacked the same spot with five or six direct hits, for now he had a plan. His hacking operation had to be halted, because the second snail was coming up behind him. Its snout and an antenna even brushed the professor's legs moistly and staggered him before he could step out of its way. Two more hatchet blows the professor got in, and then he stopped, because his right arm hurt. He had by no means gone through the shell, but he had no strength for more effort with the hatchet. He went back for his spear. His target was a small one, but he ran toward it with desperate purpose.

The blow landed. It even broke through.

The professor's hands were further torn, but he was oblivious of them. His success made him as joyous as if he had killed both his enemies, as if a rescue ship with food, water and a bed were even then sailing into Kuwa's beach.

The snail was twisting and rearing up with pain.

Professor Clavering ran forward, lifted the drooping spear and pushed it with all his might farther into the snail, pointing it upward to go as close as possible to the lung. Whether the snail died soon or not, it was *hors de combat,* the professor saw. And he himself experienced something like physical collapse an instant after seeing the snail's condition. He was quite incapable of taking on the other snail in the same manner, and the other snail was coming after him.

The professor tried to walk in a straight line away from both snails, but he weaved with fatigue and faintness. He looked behind him. The unhurt snail was thirty feet away. The wounded snail faced him, but was motionless, half in and half out of its shell, suffering in silence some agony of asphyxiation. Professor Clavering walked on.

Quite by accident, just as it was growing dark, he came upon his field of rocks. Among them he took shelter for the second time. The snail's snout probed the trench in which he lay, but could not quite reach him. Would it not be better to remain in the trench tomorrow, to hope for rain for water? He fell asleep before he could come to any decision.

Again, when the professor awakened at dawn, the snail had departed. His hands throbbed. Their palms were encrusted with dried blood and sand. He thought it wise to go to the sea and wash them in salt water.

The giant snail lay between him and the sea, and at his approach, the snail very slowly began to creep toward him. Professor Clavering made a wobbling detour and continued on his way toward the water. He dipped his hands and moved them rapidly back and forth, at last lifted water to his face, longed to wet his dry mouth, warned himself that he should not and yielded anyway, spitting out the water almost at once. Land snails hated salt and could be killed by salt crystals. The professor angrily flung handfuls of water at the snail's face. The snail only lifted its head higher, out of the professor's range. Its form was slender now, and it had, oddly, the grace of a horned gazelle, of some animal of the deer family. The snail lowered its snout, and the professor trudged away, but not quickly enough: the snail came down on his shoulder and the suctorial mouth clamped.

The professor screamed. *My God*, he thought, as a piece of his shirt, a piece of flesh and possibly bone was torn from his left shoulder, *why was I such an ass as to linger?* The snail's weight pushed him under, but it was shallow here, and he struggled to his feet and walked toward the land. Blood streamed hotly down his side. He could not bear to look at his shoulder to see what had happened, and would not have been surprised if his left arm had dropped off in the next instant. The professor walked on aimlessly in shallow water near the land. He was still going faster than the snail.

Then he lifted his eyes to the empty horizon, and saw a dark spot in the water in the mid-distance. He stopped, wondering if it were real or a trick of his eyes: but now he made out the double body of a catamaran, and he thought he saw Dr. Stead's straw hat. They had come from the Matusas!

"Hello!" The professor was shocked at the hoarseness, the feebleness of his voice. Not a chance that he had been heard.

But with hope now, the professor's strength increased. He headed for a little beach—not his beach, a smaller one—and when he got there he stood in its center, his good arm raised, and shouted, "Doctor *Stead!* This way! On the beach!" He could definitely see Dr. Stead's hat and four dark heads.

There was no answering shout. Professor Clavering could not tell if they heard him or not. And the accursed snail was only thirty feet away now! He'd lost his hatchet, he realized. And the camera that had been under water with him was now ruined, and so were the two pictures in it. No matter. He would live.

"*Here!*" he shouted, again lifting his arm.

The natives heard this. Suddenly all heads in the catamaran turned to him.

Dr. Stead pointed to him and gesticulated, and dimly Professor Clavering heard the good doctor urging the boatmen to make for the shore. He saw Dr. Stead half stand up in the catamaran.

The natives gave a whoop—at first Professor Clavering thought it a whoop of joy, or of recognition. But almost at once a wild swing of the sail, a splash of a couple of oars, told him that the natives were trying to change their course.

Pebbles crackled. The snail was near. And this of course was what the natives had seen—the giant snail.

"*Please—here!*" the professor screamed. He plunged again into the water. "*Please!*"

Dr. Stead was trying, that the professor could see. But the natives were rowing, paddling with hands even, and their sail was carrying them obliquely away.

The snail made a splash as it entered the sea. To drown or to be eaten alive, the professor wondered. He was waist-deep when he stumbled, waist-deep but head under when the snail crashed down upon him, and he realized as the thousands of pairs of teeth began to gnaw at his back, that his fate was both to drown and to be chewed to death.

Miss Pinkerton's Apocalypse

Muriel Spark

One evening, a damp one in February, something flew in at the window. Miss Laura Pinkerton, who was doing something innocent to the fire, heard a faint throbbing noise overhead. On looking up, "George! Come here! Come quickly!"

George Lake came in at once, though sullenly because of their quarrel, eating a sandwich from the kitchen. He looked up at the noise, then sat down immediately.

From this point onward their story comes in two versions, his and hers. But they agree as to the main facts; they agree that it was a small round flattish object and that it flew.

"It's a flying object of some sort," whispered George eventually.

"It's a saucer," said Miss Pinkerton, keen and loud, "an antique piece. You can tell by the shape."

"It can't be an antique, that's absolutely certain," George said.

He ought to have been more tactful, and would have been, but for the stress of the moment. Of course it set Miss Pinkerton off, she being in the right.

"I know my facts," she stated as usual. "I should hope I know my facts. I've been in antique china for twenty-three years in the autumn," which was true, and George knew it.

The little saucer was cavorting round the lamp.

"It seems to be attracted by the light," George remarked, as one might distinguish a moth.

Promptly, it made as if to dive dangerously at George's head. He ducked, and Miss Pinkerton backed against the wall. As the dish tilted on its side, skimming George's shoulder, Miss Pinkerton could see inside it.

"The thing might be radioactive. It might be dangerous." George was breathless. The saucer had climbed, was circling high above his head, and now made for him again, but missed.

"It is not radioactive," said Miss Pinkerton, "it is Spode."

"Don't be so damn silly," George replied, under the stress of the occasion.

"All right, very well," said Miss Pinkerton, "it is not Spode. I suppose you are the expert, George, I suppose you know best. I was only judging by the pattern. After the best part of a lifetime in china—"

"It must be a forgery," George said unfortunately. For, unfortunately, something familiar and abrasive in Miss Pinkerton's speech began to grind within him. Also, he was afraid of the saucer.

It had taken a stately turn, following the picture rail in a steady career round the room.

"Forgery, ha!" said Miss Pinkerton. She was out of the room like a shot, and in again carrying a pair of steps.

"I will examine the mark," said she, pointing intensely at the saucer. "Where are my glasses?"

Obligingly, the saucer settled in a corner; it hung like a spider a few inches from the ceiling. Miss Pinkerton adjusted the steps. With her glasses on she was almost her sunny self again; she was ceremonious and expert.

"Don't touch it, don't go near it!" George pushed her aside and grabbed the steps, knocking over a blue glass bowl, a Dresden figure, a vase of flowers, and a decanter of sherry; like a bull in a china shop, as Miss Pinkerton exclaimed. But she was determined, and struggled to reclaim the steps.

"Laura!" he said desperately. "I believe it is Spode. I take your word."

The saucer then flew out of the window.

They acted quickly. They telephoned to the local paper. A reporter would come right away. Meanwhile, Miss Pinkerton telephoned to her two scientific friends—at least, one was interested in psychic research and the other was an electrician. But she got no reply from either. George had leaned out of the window, scanning the rooftops and the night sky. He had leaned out of the back windows, had tried all the lights and the wireless. These things were as usual.

The newsman arrived, accompanied by a photographer.

"There's nothing to photograph," said Miss Pinkerton excitably. "It went away."

"We could take a few shots of the actual spot," the man explained.

Miss Pinkerton looked anxiously at the result of George and the steps.

"The place is a wreck."

Sherry from the decanter was still dripping from the sideboard.

"I'd better clear the place up. George, help me!" She fluttered nervously, and started to pack the fire with small coals.

"No, leave everything as it is," the reporter advised her. "Did the apparition make this mess?"

George and Miss Pinkerton spoke together.

"Well, indirectly," said George.

"It wasn't an apparition," said Miss Pinkerton.

The reporter settled on the nearest chair, poising his pencil and asking, "Do you mind if I take notes?"

"Would you mind sitting over here?" said Miss Pinkerton. "I don't use the Queen Annes normally. They are very frail pieces."

The reporter rose as if stung, then perched on a table which Miss Pinkerton looked at uneasily.

"You see, I'm in antiques," she rattled on, for the affair was beginning to tell on her, as George told himself. In fact he sized up that she was done for; his irritation abated, his confidence came flooding back.

"Now, Laura, sit down and take it easy." Solicitously he pushed her into an easy chair.

"She's overwrought," he informed the pressmen in an audible undertone.

"You say this object actually flew in this window?" suggested the reporter.

"That is correct," said George.

The cameraman trained his apparatus on the window.

"And you were both here at the time?"

"No," Miss Pinkerton said. "Mr. Lake was in the kitchen and I called out, of course. But he didn't see inside the bowl, only the outside, underneath where the manufacturer's mark is. I saw the pattern so I got the steps to make sure. That's how Mr. Lake knocked my things over. I saw inside."

"I am going to say something," said George.

The men looked hopefully towards him. After a pause, George continued, "Let us begin at the beginning."

"Right," said the reporter, breezing up.

"It was like this," George said. "I came straight in when Miss Pinkerton screamed, and there was a white convex disk, you realize, floating around up there."

The reporter contemplated the spot indicated by George.

"It was making a hell of a racket like a cat purring," George told him.

"Any idea what it really was?" the reporter inquired.

George took his time to answer. "Well, yes," he said, "and no."

"Spode ware," said Miss Pinkerton.

George continued, "I'm not up in these things. I'm extremely skeptical as a rule. This was a new experience to me."

"That's just it," said Miss Pinkerton. "Personally, I've been in china for twenty-three years. I recognized the thing immediately."

The reporter scribbled and inquired, "These flying disks appear frequently in China?"

"It was a saucer. I've never seen one flying before," Miss Pinkerton explained.

"I am going to ask a question," George said.

Miss Pinkerton continued, "Mr. Lake is an art framer. He handles old canvases but next to no antiques."

"I am going to ask. Are you telling the story or am I?" George said.

"Perhaps Mr. Lake's account first and then the lady's," the reporter ventured.

Miss Pinkerton subsided crossly while he turned to George.

"Was the object attached to anything? No wires or anything? I mean, someone couldn't have been having a joke or something?"

George gave a decent moment to the possibility.

"No," he then said. "It struck me, in fact, that there was some sort of Mind behind it, operating from outer space. It tried to attack me, in fact."

"Really, how was that?"

"Mr. Lake was not attacked," Miss Pinkerton stated. "There was no danger at all. I saw the expression on the pilot's face. He was having a game with Mr. Lake, grinning all over his face."

"Pilot?" said George. "What are you talking about—pilot!"

Miss Pinkerton sighed. "A tiny man half the size of my finger," she declared. "He sat on a tiny stool. He held the little tiny steering wheel with one hand and waved with the other. Because, there was something like a sewing machine fixed near the rim, and he worked the tiny treadle with his foot. Mr. Lake was not attacked."

"Don't be so damn silly," said George.

"You don't mean this?" the reporter asked her with scrutiny.

"Of course, I do."

"I would like to know something," George demanded.

"You only saw the underside of the saucer, George."

"You said nothing about any pilot at the time," said George. "I saw no pilot."

"Mr. Lake got a fright when the saucer came at him. If he hadn't been dodging he would have seen for himself."

"You mentioned no pilot," said George. "Be reasonable."

"I had no chance," said she. She appealed to the cameraman. "You see, I know what I'm talking about. Mr. Lake thought he knew better, however.

Mr. Lake said, 'It's a forgery.' If there's one thing I do know, it's china.''

"It would be most unlikely," said George to the reporter. "A steering wheel and a treadle machine these days, can you credit it?"

"The man would have fallen out," the cameraman reflected.

"I must say," said the reporter, "that I favor Mr. Lake's long-range theory. The lady may have been subject to some hallucination, after the shock of the saucer."

"Quite," said George. He whispered something to the photographer. "Women!" Miss Pinkerton heard him breathe.

The reporter heard him also. He gave a friendly laugh. "Shall we continue with Mr. Lake's account, and then see what we can make of both stories?"

But Miss Pinkerton had come to a rapid decision. She began to display a mood hitherto unknown to George. Leaning back, she gave way to a weak and artless giggling. Her hand fluttered prettily as she spoke between gurgles of mirth. "Oh, what a mess! What an evening! We aren't accustomed to drink, you see, and now, oh dear, oh dear!"

"Are you all right, Laura?" George enquired severely.

"Yes, yes, yes," said Miss Pinkerton, drowsy and amiable. "We really oughtn't have done this, George. Bringing these gentlemen out. But I can't keep it up, George. Oh dear, it's been fun though."

She was away into her giggles again. George looked bewildered. Then he looked suspicious.

"It's definitely the effect of this extraordinary phenomenon," George said firmly to the Press.

"It was my fault, all my fault," spluttered Miss Pinkerton.

The reporter looked at his watch. "I can quite definitely say you saw a flying object?" he asked. "And that you were both put out by it?"

"Put down that it was a small, round, flattish object. We both agree to that," George said.

A spurt of delight arose from Miss Pinkerton again.

"Women, you know! It always comes down to women in the finish," she told them. "We had a couple of drinks.

"Mr. Lake had rather more than I did," she added triumphantly.

"I assure you," said George to the reporter.

"We might be fined for bringing the Press along, George. It might be an offense," she put in.

"I assure you," George insisted to the photographer, "that we had a flying saucer less than an hour ago in this room."

Miss Pinkerton giggled.

The reporter looked round the room with new eyes; and with the air of one to whom to understand all is to forgive all, he folded his notebook. The cameraman stared at the pool of sherry, the overturned flowers, the broken glass and china. He packed up his camera, and they went away.

George gave out the tale to his regular customers. He gave both versions, appealing to their reason to choose. Further up the road at her corner shop, Miss Pinkerton smiled tolerantly when questioned.

"Flying saucer? George is very artistic," she would say, "and allowances must be made for imaginative folk." Sometimes she added that the evening had been a memorable one. "Quite a party!"

It caused a certain amount of tittering in the neighborhood. George felt this; but otherwise, the affair made no difference between them. Personally, I believe the story, with a preference for Miss Pinkerton's original version. She is a neighbor of mine. I have reason to believe this version because, not long afterwards, I too received a flying visitation from a saucer. The little pilot, in my case, was shy and inquisitive. He pedaled with all his might. My saucer was Royal Worcester, fake or not I can't say.

The Reunion After Three Hundred Years

Alexis Tolstoy

It was a balmy summer night. We were in Grandmother's garden, some of us gathered around the lamp-lit table, others settled on the terrace steps. Now and then a faint breeze fanned us with the scent of flowers or murmured the refrain of a song from the village. Soon everything became quiet, except for the night moths fluttering against the lampshade.

Well, my children, *Grandmother said,* so you want me to tell you an old ghost story. . . . If that's your wish, form a circle around me and I'll relate an incident from my youth that will leave you trembling when you are alone in your beds.

It's perfectly natural that such a calm night should remind me of the old days. You can laugh if you want, but I am so old that even nature appears less wonderful than it did at one time. Days are not as gloriously warm and sunny; flowers not as fresh nor fruit as succulent. I'll never forget the basket of peaches the Marquis d'Urfé once sent me. You know, the marquis was a young madman who courted me after falling in love with the odd little line on my forehead.

Actually, I wasn't bad-looking then. Those who now see my gray hair and wrinkles wouldn't suspect that King Louis XV used to call me the Rose of Ardennes, an appropriate name since I stuck many a thorn in His Majesty's heart.

As for the Marquis d'Urfé, I can assure you, my children, that if he had truly wanted it otherwise, I wouldn't be your grandmother and you would carry a different family name. But our coquettishness can elude men, completely causing them either to lose their heads and so disgust us, or to plunge like children into despair and exile themselves to the court of some Gospodar of Moldavia. That is exactly what happened with this mad marquis whom I encountered again many years later, though I will note *en passant* that he had still not become more sensible.

To return to the basket of peaches which the marquis gave me not long before his departure. It was Saint Ursula's Day, my saint's day, which falls in the middle of October when peaches are extremely rare. This gesture stemmed from a bet that d'Urfé had made with your grandfather who, already courting me, was so embarrassed by his rival's success that he fell ill for three days.

This marquis had the most distinguished appearance I had ever encountered—with the exception of the King, who, though getting on in years, was still the handsomest nobleman of France. In addition to the marquis' appearance, he held another attraction which, I now confess, thrilled all the young ladies: he was the most incorrigible playboy in the world. I have often wondered why, in spite of our will power, women are drawn to this type. My only explanation is that the more inconstant a man is, the more pleasant it becomes for us to tie him to our apron strings. *Amour propre* is aroused in both parties by the suspense of who will be more artful, though this game's skill lies, my dear children, in stopping before one's partner is brought to an extreme state.

I am saying this, Helen, for your sake. If you love someone, my child, don't treat him as I treated d'Urfé. God knows how I cried after his departure, how I regretted my own behavior. Your grandfather's memory need not suffer from this confession. He who married me half a year later was without any doubt the most worthy and noble man one could ever hope to meet.

Before all this began, I was widowed by the death of my first husband, the Duc de Gramont, whom I barely came to know and whom I married out of respect for my father's wishes, and because I feared to disobey him. You can easily guess that my widowhood could not last too long. I was young, good-looking and in a position to do everything I desired. I took advantage of my freedom. As soon as my period of mourning ended, I plunged into the social whirl, which, I may note, was much gayer than it is today.

At one of those gatherings, the Marquis d'Urfé was introduced to me by Commodore de Belle-Oeuvre, an old friend of my father's. My father, who never left his château in Ardennes, entrusted me to this close family friend. There was simply no end to the old commodore's admonishments. But while I reassured him as much as possible, I paid no attention to his arguments—as you shall soon see. I was familiar with d'Urfé's reputation and was anxious to find out if he was as irresistible as had been described to me.

When, with disarming ease, he first approached me, I looked so aloof that he was embarrassed and speechless.

"My lady," he later told me, "above your eyes, just over your brows, there is an almost imperceptible little line which adds indescribable power to your gaze."

"Sir," I replied, "it is said that I resemble the portrait of my great-great-grandmother Mathilde, a legendary figure whose singular gaze caused a fearless knight to fall into a moat just as he was climbing over the parapet to abduct her!"

"My lady," the marquis said with a polite bow, "if your features resemble those of your great-great-grandmother, then I accept the legend as gospel. I will go even one step further and presume to add that if I had been the knight, I would not have given up. Rather, I would have extricated myself from the moat and reclimbed the wall immediately."

"Would that have been possible, sir?"

"Without any doubt whatsoever, my lady."

"Lack of success would not have cast you into despair?"

"From time to time I can be taken aback, but to despair due to lack of success, never!"

"Well, then, sir, we will see about that."

"Yes, my dear lady, we *shall* see!"

From that moment on, a treacherous battle was waged between us: I feigned indifference while the marquis increased his tender attention. In its course, this game attracted general interest, causing Commodore de Belle-Oeuvre to reprimand me severely.

This commodore had a very original personality. Imagine for yourselves a tall, slender, distinguished gentleman, always polite and well-spoken—but never smiling. As a youth during the war he demonstrated miraculous courage that bordered on madness. Yet, ironically, he was timid with women and knew nothing of love.

Every day, true to his word, he would dispatch to my father a report regarding my behavior, as if I were still a little girl. Before the post took off, I would play up to him, transforming his frown into a funny grimace. I risked a quarrel yet couldn't keep from laughing. However, we did remain on good terms; that is, until the marquis would enter our conversations. Then he would say:

"Duchess, I am distraught because my sense of duty demands that I speak to you honestly."

"Please do, my good Commodore."

"Yesterday evening, the Marquis d'Urfé was again at your house."

"Quite right, my dear Commodore, and the day before yesterday, and tonight, as well as tomorrow and the day after tomorrow."

"It is precisely these constant visits that I wish to discuss. You well know, my lady, that your father, my highly esteemed friend, has entrusted you to my care. This makes me responsible for you before God, as if you were my own daughter . . ."

"But is it possible, my dear Commodore, that you fear the marquis will seduce me?"

"I am sure, my dear lady, the marquis approaches you with the respect that restrains him from such heinous acts. Nevertheless, it is my duty to warn you that the marquis' attentions have become the subject of discussion at court. I reproach myself for this, especially since it was I who unfortuitously introduced him to you. If you do not refrain from seeing him, I regretfully will be forced to challenge him to a duel."

"But you must be joking, my dear Commodore. How would such a duel become you? Do you forget that you're three times his age?"

"I never joke, my dear lady. Everything will happen just as I have the honor of describing it to you now."

"But, sir, this is an insult! An unmentionable tyranny! If it pleases me to be in the company of the Marquis d'Urfé, who has the right to prevent it? Who has the right to prevent him from marrying me if I should give my consent?"

"My lady," the commodore replied, shaking his head sadly, "believe me when I tell you that this does not fit into the marquis' scheme. I know life sufficiently well to see that the Marquis d'Urfé does not intend to tie himself down but only to flaunt his conquests. And what would happen to you, poor little flower of Ardennes, if you were to allow him such intimate pleasures? Surely, this charming butterfly would suddenly, heartlessly fly away."

"Well, there—you've said it. But, do you know, my dear Commodore, that if you continue this way, you will induce me to fall madly in love with this marquis?"

"I know, my dear lady, that your father, my highly esteemed friend, has placed you in my care, and I am ever prepared to anger you if only to prove myself worthy of that trust as well as your own respect."

Our arguments terminated each time in this way, though I never related them to d'Urfé for fear of further inflating his ego. One day, the commodore arrived at my house to inform me of a letter my father had sent, requesting him to escort me to our estate in Ardennes. The commodore brought another letter that was addressed to me in which Father asked to see me. So that I would not be too disappointed at the prospect of spending autumn in the isolated forests, he told me that several families in our neighborhood had planned festivities in the Château d'Oberbois, located four leagues from us.

The current occasion was a spectacular costume

ball, and Father advised me to hurry if I wished to participate in it.

The name "Oberbois" brought to mind a multitude of stories I had heard as a child about the ancient, deserted castle and its surrounding forest. Among local inhabitants, a chilling legend still flourished: that forest travelers were sometimes pursued by a gigantic, frighteningly pale, thin man who would chase carriages on all fours, attempting to grab the wheels as he howled and begged for food. Thus he was called "the famished one," also the "prior of Oberbois." I don't know why, but the image of this exhausted groveling creature had always loomed as the most horrifying specter of my imagination. Often, when I would be returning from an evening walk, I'd involuntarily cry out and squeeze my nurse's hand, for, in the twilight, the revolting creature appeared to be crawling through the trees. Father scolded me for this fantasy, but I couldn't be reassured.

The forest and the castle were connected to our family's history. During the war with the English, it all belonged to Monsieur Bertrand d'Oberbois, the very same knight who, not being able to marry my great-great-grandmother, had decided to abduct her until her gaze caused him to lose his grip on the rope ladder and fall into the moat. Monsieur Bertrand received what he deserved. He was, according to stories, a godless and perfidious knight, whose sinfulness was known throughout the land.

My great-great-grandmother's courage was remarkable, so you can understand how flattered I was when people saw my resemblance to the portrait of Madame Mathilde. You know, my children, this portrait still hangs in the large hall directly over the portrait of the Seneschal de Bourgogne, your great-great-granduncle, and next to the portrait of Seigneur Hugo de Montmorency, who became our relation in 1310.

There is reason to doubt the legend, since her portrait is so sweet and innocent, though perhaps the weakness was in the artist. Whichever is the case, I did at one time resemble the painting. But this is not what I really wanted to talk about. I have already mentioned that Monsieur Bertrand paid for his insolence by taking a bath in the moat of our castle. However, I don't know whether this affront cured him of his love. They say he tried to console himself with a group of sinners as godless and worthless as himself. He indulged in debauchery and gluttony with a certain Madame Jeanne de Rocheaigue, who pleased him by killing her husband.

I am relating what my nurse told me, my dear children, and I am only telling it because I want you to understand how frightened I always was of this revolting castle of Oberbois and how amazed I was that the costume ball was to be held there. My father's letter upset me terribly, though this was less from fear than from my unwillingness to leave Paris. The commodore, I assumed, was to quite an extent responsible for this situation. The very idea of being treated like a little girl infuriated me.

I imagined that Monsieur de Belle-Oeuvre, by

imposing this trip to Ardennes, wanted only one thing—to prevent my frequent meetings with d'Urfé. So I decided to upset his plans. When the marquis came to see me, I spoke in a mocking tone and let him think that I was leaving Paris of my own accord. This implied that he had not won my favor and consequently could not consider himself successful.

"My lady," d'Urfé answered me, "one of my châteaux, as Providence wills it, is located one league from the road upon which you will be traveling. Do I dare hope that you will not refuse to console a poor conquered creature by allowing him to offer you hospitality on your journey?"

"Sir," I coldly replied, "that would be quite a distance, and besides, why should you want to see me again?"

"I beg you, my lady, don't lead me to despair. Otherwise, I swear, I will take some extreme recourse."

"But suppose you should want to abduct me?"

"I am even capable of doing that, my lady."

At this, I burst out laughing.

"You deny the possibility?" he asked.

"Indeed, I do, sir, for such an adventure demands unswerving boldness. After all, I'll be traveling with Commodore de Belle-Oeuvre under very heavy guard!"

The marquis smiled and grew silent. Of course, I knew that the Marquis d'Urfé had an estate on the other side of Ardennes, something I had anticipated. Nevertheless, so that you will not think too badly of your grandmother, I must tell you that my challenge to the marquis was nothing but a joke. Also, I wanted to tease the commodore a bit by giving the marquis the opportunity to see me during the trip. Should the marquis have taken my words seriously, I intended to eventually confess the truth to him. Meanwhile, the prospect of seduction did not check this flirtatious and volatile young lady.

When the day for our departure finally arrived, I was shocked by the commodore's excessive precautions, excessive even by standards of that time. In addition to a carriage which was accommodated with a kitchen, there was another one for my bed and personal necessities. Stationed on the rear seats of the carriage were two footmen armed with sabers. My valet, who sat beside the driver, held a musket intended to scare away would-be robbers. A paperhanger was sent ahead in order to prepare our next night's lodgings in a proper way, while two others rode on ahead to clear the roads by day, shouting at the passers-by to give way, and to light our way with torches once it became dark.

The commodore maintained a ceremonious politeness during the trip, beginning with his sitting opposite rather than beside me.

"What's the matter with you, Commodore? Is it possible you're so afraid of me that you dare not sit next to me?"

"You can't doubt, my dear lady, my preference to sit beside the daughter of my best friend. But in so doing I might shirk my duty were I to cause the slightest discomfort to the one I have been called upon to protect."

He took his duty so seriously that every five minutes he would ask whether I was comfortable or if the wind was blowing on me.

"Will you kindly leave me in peace, my dear Commodore. You're being simply impossible!"

Then he would sigh deeply and order the driver to avoid the bumps along the road. During the day, we traveled very slowly, for the commodore insisted that I eat something at every stop. Before helping me from the carriage, he would remove his hat, give me his arm and lead me to the table. He constantly apologized for the food being inferior to the meals served in my home on the Rue Varennes.

Once, I impulsively remarked that I loved music, whereupon he ordered a guitar and sang a military song, his voice thundering and his eyes popping in an absolutely frightening way. So vigorously did he play that the strings broke.

There were as many of my own servants in our party as there were of his. The commodore had them all wear livery bearing my crest so that I would not appear to be traveling in his carriage. Yet, all this attention did not soften me because in Monsieur de Belle-Oeuvre I saw not a friend but an officious patron and pedant.

Noticing that his pockets were full of all kinds of articles designed for my well-being, I playfully pretended to need them, only to embarrass him later. At first, I didn't succeed.

Once, I exclaimed that I was nauseated. The commodore immediately put his hand into one of his pockets, produced a beautiful pill box and silently handed it to me. The next time, I feigned a headache. The commodore searched in his pockets, located a vial of *elixir vitae* and asked permission to sprinkle it on my hair. That almost discouraged me. Finally, saying I had lost my rouge, I impatiently asked Monsieur de Belle-Oeuvre whether he had thought of bringing a few jars. This made him blush deeply and extend elaborate excuses. I was even unkind enough to simulate tears, crying that I had been entrusted to a man uninterested in my welfare.

I felt partly revenged when the commodore looked disgraced and remained silently forlorn for the rest of the day. Not satisfied with just tormenting my mentor, I was busy inventing other diversions when an unexpected event interrupted the monotony of our trip.

It was evening. We were riding along the edge of a forest when a horseman wrapped in a cape suddenly appeared at a turn in the road. He peered into the window of my carriage and swiftly disappeared. It all happened so quickly that I almost didn't see the note he had tossed onto my lap. The commodore apparently did not notice. The note said the following:

You will spend the night one league from here. When everybody is asleep, a carriage will pause under your window. If you wake your people up,

I would rather die before your eyes than withdraw from the adventure of which you deem me incapable. Only its success can inject meaning into my life.

Seeing the marquis' handwriting, I gasped, causing the commodore to glance toward me.

"What's the matter, my lady?"

"Oh, nothing," I answered, hiding the note. "I suddenly had a pain in my foot."

I used this lie thirty years before *The Barber of Seville* was written, which proves that I thought it up before Beaumarchais did, contrary to what you may think.

The commodore immediately felt in his pocket and pulled out a magnet to be applied to the sore spot.

The more I pondered over the marquis' impertinence, the more I admired his knightly courage. I was grateful that I, as a woman of high birth, wore a black half-mask during the trip; otherwise the commodore might have noticed my excitement. I didn't for one moment doubt that the marquis would fulfill his intention. Being acquainted with Commodore de Belle-Oeuvre's fanaticism, however, I feared for the Marquis d'Urfé's life—and for my own good name.

The servants riding on ahead soon returned to inform us about a collapsed bridge that made it impossible to spend the night in the village selected by Monsieur de Belle-Oeuvre. Our head steward had already prepared a supper at the next hunting lodge, situated near the highway and belonging to Monsieur the Marquis d'Urfé. When he heard this name, the commodore's face darkened, and I became worried that he would divine the marquis' plan.

Fortunately, he did not, so we arrived at the hunting lodge without any suspicions whatsoever. After supper, he bowed as he did every evening, asked permission to retire and wished me a restful sleep.

After he left, I dismissed the maids and decided not to undress, since I shortly expected the Marquis d'Urfé's appearance. I resolved to treat him the way he deserved, yet without bringing the commodore's wrath upon him.

An hour had barely passed when I heard a slight rustle in the courtyard. Opening the window, I saw the marquis climbing toward me on a rope ladder.

"Sir, leave at once or I will call my people!"

"Have mercy, my lady, and hear me out."

"I don't want to listen to anything, and if you try to enter, I promise to ring the bell!"

"Then order me killed, for I have made an oath that only death can prevent me from abducting you!"

I didn't know what to answer, when suddenly the window of the next room opened, revealing the commodore, lamp in hand. Monsieur de Belle-Oeuvre had changed into a dark red robe and his hat was replaced by a sharply pointed nightcap. There was something impressive about his appearance, like that of a whimsical magician.

"Marquis!" he boomed, "would you kindly remove yourself from here!"

"Monsieur Commodore," the marquis answered, still hanging on to the rope ladder, "I am pleased to have you in my house."

"Monsieur Marquis," continued the commodore, "I must inform you that if you don't get down at once, I will have the honor of shooting you!"

Saying this, he placed the lamp on the window sill and aimed two huge pistols at the marquis.

"What is wrong with you, Commodore!" I shrieked, sticking my head out the window. "That would be murder!"

"Duchess," Monsieur de Belle-Oeuvre bowed politely, "be so gracious as to forgive me for presenting myself before you in such unsuitable attire, but in these unusual circumstances I pray your indulgence. Also be so kind as to forgive me for not obeying you with that blind zeal I have always considered binding. But your father, my highly esteemed friend, has committed you to my care, and his trust is so flattering that I am prepared to defend it at any price, including murder."

With these words, the commodore again bowed, then loaded his pistols.

"All right!" the marquis said, "this will be a new kind of duel!" And without descending the rope ladder, he also produced a pair of pistols. "Commodore, please put out the lamp; it makes my position superior to yours. I cannot take advantage of you in this way."

"Monsieur Marquis, I thank you for your courtesy and am glad to see your pistols, since I could not shoot an unarmed man." He extinguished his lamp and aimed at the marquis.

"Both of you have gone mad!" I cried. "You are going to ruin me. You will waken the entire house! Marquis, I forgive you for your indiscretion, but only on the condition that you climb down immediately. Do you hear, sir? I order you to get down!"

My expression must have conveyed to him that any delay would only make me angrier.

"My lady," he said, referring to the conversation of our first meeting, "your gaze makes me descend this ladder. Yet the reigning beauty, Mathilde, should be assured that Knight Bertrand will seek another meeting with her, if only to die at her feet!" Wrapping himself in his cape, he thus vanished into the darkness.

Next day, the commodore refrained from mentioning this occurrence, nor did we ever speak about it again.

When my father's château remained only half a day's ride away, we were caught by such a horrible storm that in spite of closed eyelids, the ferocious lightning blinded me.

You know, my children, I have never tolerated electric storms. Some incomprehensible fear overtakes me and I tremble like a leaf. That evening, I huddled against the commodore, who kept apologizing for the elements.

We were proceeding very slowly, being hindered

by fallen trees. It was completely dark when the driver halted the horses abruptly and addressed the commodore:

"I am sorry, sir, but I have driven in the wrong direction. We are in the forest of Oberbois. I recognize it by that old oak with the severed branches." He barely had time to utter these words when a crash of thunder shook the whole forest, and lightning struck near the carriage. The terrified horses went wild.

"Mother of God, have mercy on us!" exclaimed the driver, winding the reins around his hands. But the horses didn't obey.

We were careening along from right to left, at full speed, expecting at any moment to crash into a tree.

I was dazed and couldn't understand anything Monsieur de Belle-Oeuvre said. The wind and thunder made eerie sounds. Several times I heard heartrending moans and then a piercing howl: "I want food. I want food." Suddenly the driver, who was trying to restrain the horses, dropped the reins and, with a horrible scream, started to whip them.

"Germain, you scoundrel!" the commodore shouted. "Have you gone mad?"

Germain turned his head and a flash of lightning lit up his deathly pale face.

"It is the prior!" he said in a hollow voice. "The prior is chasing us."

"Stop the horses, you idiot. It will be your own fault if the duchess breaks her head! Stop, or I'll have you shot."

Monsieur de Belle-Oeuvre had hardly finished his sentence when we felt a terrific jolt. I was hurled from the carriage and lost consciousness. I don't know how long I lay thus, but I awakened to the sound of music coming from some place nearby. I opened my eyes to find myself lying on some moss, surrounded by the forest.

The storm had ended, but thunder echoed from time to time in the distance, and the leaves quietly trembled on the trees. The air was heavy with an aroma that submerged me in sweet lethargy. A few drops of rain water falling on my face from the leaves above revived me.

I sat up and saw brightly lit vaulted windows about a hundred steps away. Beyond the trees I could see pointed turrets belonging to an unfamiliar castle. "Where am I?" I wondered, then recalled how the horses had gone wild, causing me to be thrown from the carriage. I was so dizzy that these fragmented recollections mixed with others. Nor did my aloneness surprise me. I didn't even notice the absence of Monsieur de Belle-Oeuvre and my servants.

The music which had revived me was still audible. "Possibly I am near the castle of Oberbois," I thought, "and the guests are gathering for the costume ball my father had mentioned in his letter." I recalled the Marquis d'Urfé's last words and was certain that with his determination, he would certainly be present at this ball.

I rose and, not feeling any pain, went quickly toward the castle. It was a huge, partially decayed, forbidding structure, with moss- and ivy-covered walls. Branches hung like garlands from high towers, gracefully swaying, their outlines silhouetted against the silvery-blue background of the night sky. I stopped for a moment to admire the view. For some reason my mind wandered to my childhood. Lucid images passed before my eyes, among them the picture of my mother smiling sadly after presenting me with a cross. I felt like crying and several times kissed the little cross from which I was never parted.

Suddenly the commodore's voice called me from somewhere in the distance. I strained to hear it but a weather vane squeaked like grinding teeth. Deciding it was only my imagination, I entered the court. No carriages or servants were visible, though loud voices and laughter could be heard. I ascended a very steep but brightly lit stairway. At the head of the top landing, a cold wind whipped past my face. A frightened owl flapped her wings from side to side, hitting against the wall lamps.

To avoid the bird's wings, I crouched on the marble floor. When I straightened up, a tall knight in full armor stood before me, extending his hand in a mailed glove. Under the lowered visor, a hollow voice murmured: "My lovely lady, allow your faithful servant to receive you in his castle which you must consider, along with everything in it, your own."

I remembered the words uttered by the Marquis d'Urfé when I had ordered him to retreat from the rope ladder. Being certain that this unidentified knight was none other than the gallant gentleman, I answered accordingly.

"Don't be surprised, my excellent sire, by seeing me here. Having lost my way in the forest, I came to you for the hospitality consonant with all brave and noble knights."

I entered a large hall filled with people, all of whom were laughing and singing around tables piled high with food and drink. They were dressed like noblemen at the Court of Charles VII and like people in the paintings in the church of St. Germain in Auxerre. I had seen paintings from that period and could appreciate the historical accuracy of their costumes.

More than anything else, my attention was attracted by the coiffure of a tall and ravishing lady, apparently the hostess of this festivity. Her hair was covered with a net tastefully and elegantly woven out of gold threaded with pearls. In spite of her beauty, however, this lady had a wicked expression.

As I entered, she studied me with impertinent curiosity and said in a voice loud enough for me to hear: "If I am not mistaken, this is the charming Mathilde for whom Monsieur Bertrand unsuccessfully longed—that is, until he joined with me!"

Then, turning to the knight, she said caustically, "My heart, order this lady to leave if you don't want me to become jealous!"

This joke sounded particularly coarse to me, especially since I was not acquainted with the woman who permitted herself the freedom of speaking to me thus. I wanted to make an appropriate rejoinder and was ready to address Monsieur the Marquis d'Urfé, when a din arose among the guests.

They were speaking to one another, raising their eyebrows, winking and pointing at me in turn.

The lady who had spoken to the knight reached for a lamp and approached me so quickly that she seemed to be floating, not walking. Lifting the lamp high, she directed everyone's attention to my shadow.

Screeches of revulsion reverberated from all sides, and the same words were repeated by each member of the crowd: "Look at the shadow! Look at the shadow! She is not one of us."

At first I didn't understand the significance of these words, but after examining the throng, I realized with horror that no one else was casting a shadow. They were all gliding past the torches, their transparent bodies not screening the flames.

Inexpressible fear seized me. Feeling faint, I put my hand to my heart. My fingers touched the little cross which I had recently kissed, and again I seemed to hear the commodore calling me. I wanted to flee, but the knight clasped my hand in his mailed fist, forcing me to remain.

"Don't be afraid. I swear by the damnation of my soul that I will not permit anyone to hurt you. And so that no one should even consider it, the priest will bless and marry us at once."

The crowd receded as a wan and scrawny monk crawled toward us on all fours. He looked as if he were tormented by cruel pains. In response to his moans, the lady with the netted pearls laughed unnaturally and turned to the knight.

"You see, sir; you see that our prior is being as stubborn as he was three hundred years ago!"

The knight raised his visor. His face, not at all like d'Urfé's, was livid, and his gaze conveyed such bestial cruelty that I could not endure it. His eyes, popping out of their sockets, were riveted on me. The prior crawled on the floor, murmuring prayers which were occasionally interrupted by such horrible curses and cries of pain that my hair stood on end. Cold beads of perspiration formed on my forehead. I was in no position to escape because Monsieur Bertrand's group prevented me from moving. All I could do was look and listen.

When the monk finally turned to those present and began to announce my marriage to Monsieur Bertrand d'Oberbois, my consuming dread and indignation endowed me with supernatural strength. With a sharp wrench, I freed my hand and held my cross over the ghosts.

"Whoever you may be," I exclaimed, "in the name of the eternal God I order you to vanish!"

At these words, Monsieur Bertrand's face turned blue. He swayed to and fro. Loudly, like an iron kettle, his armor crashed to the floor. Simultaneously, all the other ghosts disappeared and a gust of wind extinguished the lights.

Now I was in the midst of the ruins of this sprawling castle. The moon shining through one of the vaulted windows seemed to illuminate a crowd of self-flagellating monks, but even this vision dissolved once I made the sign of the cross. I could still hear the dying sounds of their prayers; I could distinguish the words: "Food, food, give me food!" until they were only an echo in my ears.

Overcome by fatigue, I fell into a deep slumber. When I came to, I was being carried by a man who, with big strides, was stepping over tree stumps and bushes. In the mist of the early dawn, I recognized the commodore, his clothing torn and smeared with blood.

"My lady," he said to me when he realized I had regained consciousness, "if the most cruel moment of my life occurred when I lost you, then I assure you that nothing at the present time could compare with my happiness were it not poisoned by the thought that I was unable to prevent your fall."

"Stop feeling so wretched, dear Commodore, and please put me down. I am exhausted, but judging from the way you are carrying me, you could never make a good wet nurse!"

"If that is so, my dear lady, then blame not my zeal but my broken left arm!"

"My God! How did you break it?"

"When I threw myself after you, dear lady, as duty required when I saw that the daughter of my highly esteemed friend had been thrown from the carriage."

Though touched by Monsieur de Belle-Oeuvre's devotion, I convinced him to let me walk by myself. I also offered to make a bandage for him out of my handkerchief, but he said his condition did not warrant such concern, that he was more than happy to have one good arm with which to serve me.

We hadn't reached the forest's edge when we were met by servants sent by my father when he had learned about the accident from our servants. He was conducting a search himself in a different direction. When we were reunited, my father was overcome with relief and joy. He tried to embrace Monsieur de Belle-Oeuvre, whom he hadn't seen in years. But the commodore stepped back, saying very seriously:

"My dear sir and most beloved friend, you have touched me deeply by entrusting me with your daughter, your most precious possession. But I have proven myself unworthy of this honor, for, in spite of all my efforts, I could not prevent the thunder that frightened our horses, the carriage that broke, or the fall that your daughter suffered in the midst of the forest. So you see, kind sir and dear friend, I have not vindicated your trust, and since it is only right that I give you satisfaction, I offer to fight with either sword or pistol. Due to the condition of my left arm, I regretfully cannot use a dagger, a weapon you may prefer. I know you are too fair to reproach me for a lack of good will. As for the duel, I am at your service whenever and wherever you should choose."

My father was astounded and managed only with the greatest effort to convince the commodore that he had done everything in his power under impossible circumstances, and that there were absolutely no grounds for a duel.

Monsieur de Belle-Oeuvre embraced my father

warmly, ecstatic at his decision.

I asked the commodore to tell us how he had found me. He said he had thrown himself after me but, in so doing, had hit his head against a tree and lost consciousness for some time. Coming to, he discovered his broken left arm, though this did not deter him from searching for me while he continually called my name. Finally, after an arduous search, he discovered my unconscious body among the castle ruins, from which he carried me in his right arm.

I, in turn, recounted what had taken place in the castle of Oberbois, though my father interpreted it all as either a bad dream or a trick of the imagination. I took his jests into serious consideration, yet, deep in my heart, I was thoroughly convinced of the validity of my experience. Besides, there was still a strong ache in my hand which had been pressed by Knight Bertrand's mailed fist.

All this frenzy made me ill, forcing me to spend more than two feverish weeks in bed.

During this time, my father and the commodore, whose arm was being treated by a local surgeon, were either playing chess in my room, or searching through a huge chest filled with ancient papers.

Once, when I was lying awake with my eyes shut, I heard my father tell the commodore: "Here, read this, my friend, and give me your opinion."

Growing curious, I half opened my eyes and saw my father holding a faded parchment from which several wax seals hung—the same kind that customarily appear on parliamentary decrees and royal edicts of former times.

The commodore read the parchment in a low voice, often turning in my direction. It was a message from King Charles VII to all the barons in Ardennes announcing and declaring the royal seizure of estates belonging to Knight Bertrand d'Oberbois and Madame Jeanne de Rocheaigue, both convicted of ungodly crimes.

The edict began with the usual formalities:

We, Charles the Seventh, by the Grace of God, King of France, convey our affection to all those who read this decree. To all our Vassals, Barons, Seigneurs, Knights and Noblemen let it be known that our aides have informed us that our Baron, Monsieur Knight Bertrand d'Oberbois, has slyly and spitefully been guilty of insubordination and has opposed our royal authority . . .

Then followed a long list of Knight Bertrand's misdemeanors, including sacrilegious thoughts and conduct toward the holy church:

. . . by willfully not respecting it or observing its fasts; by singing; by not confessing or accepting communion of the blood and flesh of our Lord and Savior Jesus Christ.

And so this Knight has conducted himself in the most blasphemous way possible; for even on the night of the Assumption of our most Holy Mistress, the Mother of God, he glutted himself at a vile feast.

It has been attested that Monsieur Bertrand himself said: "I swear by the damnation of my soul that I do not at all believe in eternal life. Yet, if it be so, at the cost of relinquishing my soul to Satan, I intend in three hundred years from this day to return to my castle for rejoicing at a feast. To this promise I swear and give my oath."

As the edict stated, these insolent words had such an effect upon the other participants at the feast that they also made an oath to meet in exactly three hundred years to that day and hour in the castle of Knight Bertrand. For this act they were pronounced heretics and pagans.

Very soon after the pronouncement of such terrible deeds, Knight Bertrand was found, evidently choked to death or suffocated by his armor, thereby relinquishing him from punishment for his crimes. Still, his estates were confiscated, along with the possessions of his accomplice and friend, Madame Jeanne de Rocheaigue. She, a charming demon, was accused of ruining the prior of a certain monastery, after having exploited him in the murder of her husband. She had killed this unworthy priest in a monstrous manner: ordering him hamstrung and then thrown, crippled, into the forest of Oberbois:

and it was pitiful to come upon him as he crawled and contorted himself until perishing miserably from hunger in the forest.

*   *   *   *   *

The end of the edict mentioned that one of our ancestors was, by the King's decree, to possess the castles formerly owned by Knight Bertrand and Madame Jeanne.

When the commodore completed his reading, Father asked him for the exact date of our arrival.

"It was on the night of the Assumption of the Holy Virgin. That night I had the misfortune first to lose, then happily redeem the duchess, your daughter."

"The edict is dated 1459," my father said, "and it is now 1759. That means exactly three hundred years have passed since the evening of the knight's feast. But let us not, my dear Commodore, inform my daughter of this. It is far better that she think it all a dream."

At these words, I felt overcome with horror. Noticing my behavior, Father and the commodore exchanged worried glances. But I pretended to have just awakened and feigned weakness.

In a few days, I had completely recovered. Soon afterward, I left for Paris, again escorted by Monsieur de Belle-Oeuvre. I found d'Urfé to be more deeply in love with me than ever before. But clinging to the damnable habit of coquetry, I behaved even more coldly and continued to torment him and jest at his expense, especially about his unsuccessful abduction. So well did I fare that one morning he came to tell me of his decision to go to Moldavia. He had tired of our game.

Half a year after the marquis' departure, I married your grandfather. I must admit, my children, that

I took this step at least partially from sorrow. Nevertheless, as they say, love-marriages are not always the best ones. After all, your grandfather, whom I had always respected, brought me considerably more happiness than the marquis ever could have. He really was a flighty person, a fact which nevertheless did not prevent me from finding him a very charming man.

The Attic Express

Alex Hamilton

In the evenings they climbed the steep narrow stairway to the big room under the roof. Hector Coley
went up eagerly and alertly. The boy followed his
father draggingly. In the family it had always been
called "Brian's room," but to Brian it seemed that
his father's presence filled it.

It was a long room, with low side walls and a
ceiling like the lower half of an A. There was a large
water tank at one end. The rest of the space was
"Brian's."

Coley ran the trains. The boy looked on.

Sometimes, when his father was absorbed, attending to midget couplings, rearranging a length
of track, wiring up a tiny house so that it could be
lit from inside, he looked away and merely watched
the single square of attic window gently darken.

Coley hated Brian to lose interest. He would say

irritably: "I can't understand you, Brian; beggared if I can! You know something? Some boys would give an arm to have the run of a playroom like this one I've built for you."

The boy would shift his gaze and rub his hands together nervously. He would stoop forward hastily and peer at all parts of the track. "Make it go through the crossing," he would say, to appease his father. But even before the magnificent little Fleischmann engine challenged the gradient to the crossing—which would involve the delicious maneuver of braking two or three small cars—his eye would be away again, after a moth on the wall, or a cloud veiling the moon.

"It defeats me," Coley would say later to his wife. "He shows no interest in anything. Sometimes I don't get a word out of him all evening unless I drag it out of him."

"Perhaps he's not old enough yet," she would reply diffidently. "You know, I think I'd find it a little difficult to manage myself—all those signals and control switches and lights going on and off and trains going this way and that way. I'm glad I'm never asked to work out anything more complicated than a Fair Isle knitting pattern."

"You miss the point," said Coley impatiently. "I'm not expecting him to synchronize the running times of ten trains, and keep them all safely on the move, but I would like a spark of enthusiasm to show now and again. I mean, I give up hours of my time, not to speak of money running into thousands, to give him a layout which I'm willing to wager a couple of bob can't be matched in any home in Britain. And he can't even do me the courtesy of listening to me when I explain something. It's not good enough."

"I know, dear, how you feel, but at ten I do feel it may be a little . . ."

"Oh, rubbish!" exclaimed Coley. "Ten's a helluvan age. At ten I could dismantle a good watch and put it together again better than new."

"You are exceptional, dear. Not everyone has your mechanical bent. I expect Brian's will show itself in time."

"There again, will it? His reports all read the same: 'Could do much better if he applied himself more . . . doesn't get his teeth into it . . .' and so on till I could give him a jolly good hiding. No, Meg, say what you like, it's plain to me that the boy simply won't try."

"In some subjects he's probably a little better than in others."

"Nonsense," said Coley energetically. "Anybody can do anything, if they want to enough."

One evening, after listening to his complaints meekly for a while, she suddenly interrupted him:

"Where is he now?"

"Where I left him. I've given him the new express in its box. I want to see whether he's got enough gumption to set it out on the track with the right load. If I find it's still in the box when I get back . . ."

"Yes, dear," she said, surprising him with her vehemence. "Why don't you bring the matter to a head? It's getting on my nerves a bit, you know, to be down here reading and watching television, and to imagine you struggling. If he's not really interested, then could we have an end to all this? I know the railways are your pride, but honestly I'd rather see them scrapped than listen to any more of this."

He was astonished. He went back upstairs without a word.

The boy was squatting, with his face cupped in one hand, elbow on knee. His straight brown hair fell forward and half obscured his face. The other arm dangled loosely, and the forefinger of his hand moved an empty light truck to and fro a few inches on the floor.

The express was on the rails. Brian had it at the head of an extraordinary miscellaneous collection of wagons: Pullmans, goods trucks, restaurant cars, breakdown wagons, timber trucks, oil canisters— anything, obviously, which had come to hand.

"Sit down at the control panel, Brian," snapped Coley.

The boy did not reply, but he did what he was told.

"I want you to run this express tonight," said Coley, "and I'm not going to lift a finger to help. But I'll be fair, too. I won't criticize. I'll stay right out of it. In fact, for all you know I might as well be on the train itself. Think of me being on it, that's it, and run it accordingly . . ."

He was trying to keep the anger and disappointment out of his voice. The boy half turned a moment and looked at him steadily. Then he resumed his scrutiny of the control panel.

". . . take your time . . . think it all out . . . don't do anything hastily . . . keep your wits about you . . . remember all I've taught you . . . that's a gorgeous little model I've got there for you . . . I'm on board . . . up on the footplate if you like . . . we'll have a gala and just have it lit with the illuminations of the set itself . . . give me time to get aboard . . . I'm in your hands, son . . ."

Coley stood on the railway line. The giant express faced him, quiet, just off the main line. He started to walk along the track towards it.

He felt no astonishment at finding himself in scale with the models. *Anyone can do anything, if they want to enough.* He'd wished to drive a model, from the footplate, and here he was walking towards it.

But at the first step he took he sank almost up to his knees in the ballast below the track. It was, after all, only foam rubber. He grinned. "I'll have to remember things like that," he told himself.

He stopped by the engine and looked up at the boiler. He whistled softly between his teeth, excited by so much beauty. What a lovely job these Germans made of anything they tackled. Not a plate out of line. A really sumptuous, genuine, top-of-the-form job! He wished the maker a ton of good dinners. The thing was real, not a doubt.

He stepped on through tiny, incisive pebbles of sand, treading cautiously. One or two had threatened to cut into his shoes. Looking down, he noticed a right-angled bar of metal, gleaming at his feet. He realized in a moment that it must be one of the staples which had held the engine's box together. Chuckling over his own drollness at playing the game to the full, he picked up the bar and with an effort almost succeeded in straightening it right out.

Then he advanced on the wheel and tapped it. The wheel was, of course, sound. He ran his hand over the virgin wheel. He lifted his arm and placed his hand against the smooth gloss of the boiler. He could do that because it was quite cold. He smiled again: that took away a bit of the realism, to think of a steam engine run on electricity. When you were down to scale it seemed you noticed these things.

Then he frowned as he noticed something else. The coupling of the first carriage, a Pullman, could not have been properly made up by Brian. The first wheels were well clear of the rails. He ran past the tender to have a look. Sure enough. Damn careless of him! He was about to call out to Brian when he remembered his promise to say nothing, and thought he'd make the correction himself. It was just a matter of sliding the arm across until the spoke fell into the slot in the rear of the tender. The remainder of the fastening was simple. He jabbed the lever in under the arm and strained to shift the carriage.

After a minute, during which the carriage swayed a bit but did not move, he stopped and took off his coat. He was still in his office suit. He wished he were in his old flannels and lumberjack shirt, but at least he hadn't changed into slippers. Sweat trickled down his back. He hadn't had much time for exercise lately, though his usual practice was conditioning on the links, alternate fifteen yards running and walking, for eighteen holes. Without clubs, of course.

He hurled himself at it again, bracing his full weight against the lever. Suddenly the arm shifted and skidded over the new surface on which it rested. The spoke found the slot, and the whole carriage crashed into position on the rails. The lever flicked off with rending force, and one spinning end struck him under the arm, just near the shoulder.

He thought he would be sick with pain. All feeling went out of his arm, except at the point of impact. There was plenty of feeling, all vividly unpleasant. Almost mechanically he leaned down and picked up his jacket. Trailing it, he tottered back to the engine and slowly hoisted himself into the cab. There he leaned over one of the immobile levers until he had partially recovered.

He was still palpating his startled flesh, and establishing that no bone was broken, when, without any preliminary warning, the train suddenly jerked into motion. Wheeling round, he managed to save himself from falling by hooking himself into the window of the cab. He looked for his son, to signal he was not quite ready yet. Even without the blow he had just sustained he would have liked a few more minutes to adjust himself to the idea of being part of a model world before the journey began.

But he couldn't at first see where he was. In this

fantastic landscape, lit but not warmed by three suns, all the familiar features had undergone a change. The sensation resembled in some way that which comes to a man who visits a district he knows well by daylight for the first time after dark.

In the direct light of those three suns, an overhead monster and two wall brackets, everything glittered. Plain to Coley, but less noticeable to the boy at the table on which was spread the control panel, were separate shadows of differing intensity radiating from every upright object. But the objects themselves sparkled. Light came flashing and twinkling and glancing from the walls and roofs of the houses, from the foliage of the trees, from the heaps of coal by the sidings, from the clothes and faces of the men and women. The lines of the railway themselves shone, twisting and turning a hundred times amongst windmills and farms and garages and fields and stations, all throwing back this aggressive, stupefying brilliance of light. Coley screwed up his eyes and tried to work it out.

The train slipped forward smoothly, gaining momentum. The boy hadn't made a bad job of the start, anyway. Perhaps he took in more than I imagined, said Coley to himself.

He fixed his eye on a vast gray expanse, stretching away parallel to the course they were on, and appearing like a long rectangular field of some kind of close undergrowth with curling tops. What the devil could that be? He didn't remember putting down anything like that. Whatever it was, it didn't look anything like the real thing, now that he was down to scale. A breeze stirred small clumps which seemed to ride clear of the rest, and it came to him that, of course, this was the strip of carpet he'd laid down on one side of the room, always insisting that people should walk only on this if possible, to prevent breakages.

If that was the carpet . . . he rushed across to the other window, just in time before the engine started to take a corner, to see the top of his son's head, bent over the controls.

It was miles away! So huge! So . . . dare he admit it to himself . . . grotesque! The line of his parting, running white across his scalp, showed to the man in the cab like a streak in a forest, a blaze consequent upon road-making. A house could have been hidden behind the hair falling across his forehead. The shadow of his son on the burning white sky behind was like a storm cloud.

Brian disappeared from his view as the track curled, and Coley shook his head, as if he could clear away these images as a dog rattles away drops of water from its fur. "It's not like me to imagine things," said Coley fiercely. All the same, beads of moisture stood out on the back of the hand which clutched a lever.

He sensed a slight acceleration. The telegraph poles were coming by now at more than one a second. He felt the use of his injured arm returning, and with it a return of self-confidence. "I wonder if, when I return to my normal size, the bruise will be to scale or be only, quite literally, a scratch?"

He was about to resume his jacket, since the wind

was now considerable, when the train turned again and he lost his balance. In falling, the jacket fell from his hand and was whipped away out of the cab.

Unhurt by his fall, but irritated by the loss of the jacket, Coley pulled himself to his feet and swore: "Helluva lot of bends on this railway," as if he were perceiving it for the first time. "Anyway, that doesn't matter so much. I can put up with a fresh wind for a while if he'd only think what all this bloody light is doing to my eyes. Tone down the ruddy glare, can't you?"

As if in answer, the suns were extinguished.

For an instant the succeeding blackness was complete.

The express forged almost noiselessly through the dark. Coley fumbled for handholds. "That's a bit inefficient," he muttered. But the totality of darkness was not for long. Simultaneously, and Coley imagined Brian studying the switches, all the lights in the houses and stations and farms and windmills, and so forth, were flipped on.

"That's really rather nice to look at!" said Coley appreciatively. "I always knew I'd done a good job there, but it's only now that I can see just how good. I don't think they can complain there," he went on. "I think they'd admit I've looked after that little creature comfort." He was referring to the little people with whom he had populated the world in which the attic express was running.

He also thought, as the walls of the attic vanished altogether: "If he hasn't noticed that the old man's no longer sitting in the armchair behind him, he's not likely to now. It would be rather good to slip back into the chair before the lights go up again. I'll have to watch my moment as soon as he's had enough and stops the express."

They sped through a crossing. Coley, looking down on it, and at the figures massed by the gate, observed a solitary figure in a patch of light, waving. Whimsically, he waved back. The expression on the face of the waving man was one of jubilation. His smile reached, literally, from ear to ear. "A cheery chappie," remarked Coley. He was beginning to enjoy himself.

At a comfortable pace the express swung into a long straight which led into the area described on the posters and signboards as Coleyville. It was the largest and best equipped of the five stations. Coley thought that Brian must see it as an inevitable stop. Interesting to see whether he could bring it in to a nice easy check. The passengers might be assumed to be taking down their suitcases, and dragging on their coats, and would be resentful at being over-balanced.

Far up ahead Coley could see the platform approaching. He could make out the long line of people waiting to climb aboard. "A representative body of folk," thought Coley. "I got in a good cross-section of the traveling public for Coleyville." Then, flashing down the hill, on the road which would cross the track just this side of the station in a scissors intersection, Coley saw an open sports car. It was coming down at a frightening speed, and should reach the junction just as the express went through.

"The young monkey!" breathed Coley. "He must be getting into the swing of it." For a moment he tensed, until he remembered that on this crossing there was a synchronization which would automatically brake the car. A high, whining, metallic noise filled his ears from the single rail of the roadster, which abruptly cut off as the car was stopped.

"From eighty to rest in a split second," thought Coley. "That's not too realistic. Not the boy's fault, but I'll have to see if I can't improve on that." He also noticed, as the express moved slowly through the crossing, that there were no features on the face of the roadster's driver. Not even eyes! "No use telling you to look where you're going!" shouted Coley. The square-shouldered driver sat upright and motionless, waiting for the express to be out of his way.

The express stopped at Coleyville.

"Perfect!" exclaimed Coley. "Just perfect!" He wished he could shake Brian's hand. The boy must care, after all, to be able to handle the stuff in this way. His heart swelled. He thought for a moment of stepping off at Coleyville and watching from the outside for a while, and then picking her up again next time she stopped. But he couldn't be sure the boy would bring her round again on the same line. And this was far too exhilarating an adventure to duck out of now. He stayed.

He leaned out of the cab and looked down the platform at the people waiting. It was a mild surprise to him that no one moved. There they stood, their baggage in their hands or at their feet, waiting for trains, and doing nothing about it when one came. He saw the guard, staring at him. The guard's face was a violent maroon color, and the front part of one foot was missing. He had doubtless good reasons for drinking heavily. Immediately behind him was a lovely blond, about seven feet high, and with one breast considerably larger than the other, but otherwise delicious to look at. At her side was a small boy in suit and school cap. He had the face of a middle-aged man. Farther on down, a toothless mastiff gamboled, at the end of a leash held by a gentleman in city suit and homburg. He was flawless but for the fact that he had omitted to put on collar and tie.

Coley rubbed the side of his nose with his index finger. "I never expected to discover that you had such curious characters," he said ruefully. The guard stared at him balefully, the blond proudly. The express moved out of the station. Coley took his shoe off and hammered the glass out of the right-hand foreport. It was too opaque for proper vision. He smiled as he thought of the faces of the makers if he should write to them criticizing. Being Germans, they'd take it seriously, and put the matter right in future.

Beyond Coleyville the track wound through low hills. Coleyville was a dormitory town, but on the outskirts were some prosperous farms whose flocks could be seen all about the hills. A well-appointed country club lay at the foot of the high land which bordered the east wall, which was continued in illusion by a massive photograph of the Pennines which Coley had blown up to extend most of the length of the wall. It was, in Coley's view, one of the most agreeable and meticulously arranged districts in his entire layout.

By the fences of the farms stood children, waving. Yokels waved. Lambs and dogs frisked. A water mill turned slowly. It ran on a battery, but looked very real. Plump milkmaids meandered to and fro. "Lovely spot for a holiday," thought urban Coley sentimentally. He leaned far out of the cab window to have a better view of the whole wide perspective, and almost had his head taken off by a passing goods train.

It came up very softly, passing on the outside of a curve. Coley withdrew his head only because he happened to catch a slight shadow approach.

He leaned his face against the cold metal by his window.

"Idiot!" he said to himself in fright and anger.

The goods train went by at a smart clip. There were only about five trucks on it, all empty.

"Steady, old chap!" he apostrophized his son, under his breath. "Don't take on too much all at once."

For the first time it occurred to him that it might be a good thing to be ready to skip clear in the event of danger. Brian was operating very sensibly at present, but a lapse in concentration . . . a vague chill passed down Coley's spine.

He looked back at the train on which he was

traveling. It might be better to pick his way to the rear coaches.

He took three strides and launched himself onto the tender. Landing, he tore his trousers on the rough surface which represented coal lumps. It was very slippery and he almost slid right over it altogether, but he contrived to dig toes and hands into the depressions and check himself.

The express was moving along an embankment. Below him he could see the figures of young women in bathing suits disporting themselves about a glass swimming pool. Uniformed waiters stood obsequiously about, handing drinks to shirt-sleeved gentlemen under beach umbrellas. In the context of nighttime the scene appeared macabre and hinting of recondite pleasures, particularly when the white legs of one of the beauties, protruding from under a glittering russet bush, were taken into account. She could have been a corpse, and none of the high-lifers caring.

Coley wriggled forward cautiously over the hard black lumps. He wished now he'd stayed where he was, since the strong wind was more than he had allowed for.

He scrambled to a sitting position on the hard, pointed surface of the tender. Beyond the country club, looking ahead, were the mountains. He sought about for the secure footholds he'd need before making his leap off the tender into the gaping doorway of the Pullman behind, but decided to postpone the effort until the express had passed through the long tunnel. There was a long gentle declivity on the far side—a gradient of 1:248 he'd posted it—and he'd have a more stable vehicle to jump to. Besides, in the tunnel it would be dark.

He remembered himself one Sunday morning making the mountain secure above the tunnel. The trouble he'd had with that material, nailing it in firmly without damaging any of the features of the landscape built on to it.

Those nails!

Some must protrude into the tunnel itself! He'd never troubled himself about them. There had always been plenty of clearance for the trains themselves. But for him, perched on top of the tender? He looked round desperately to see if he might still have time to make his leap.

But he remembered too late. The tunnel sucked them in like a mouth. He rolled flat on his face and prayed.

It was not completely dark, though very nearly so. A vague glow came through at one section where a tricky bit of building had been finally effected with painted canvas, and in it he was lucky to spot one of the nails and wriggle clear. The other he never saw. The point, aimed perpendicularly downwards, just caught his collar, as it arched upward over his straining neck.

He was jerked up bodily. It was very swift. He had no time to do anything about it. For a second he seemed to be suspended on the very tip of the nail, then the shirt tore and he was delivered back on the train.

He landed with a vicious thump on some part of a wagon some distance below roof level. Something drove like the tip of a boot into his knee and he doubled over against what might be a rail. He clung to it. He couldn't tell where he was, but he could hear a wheel clicking furiously beneath him. Gasping from the pain of his knee, and a dull throb between the shoulder blades, he hung on and waited for the end of the tunnel and light.

It came suddenly.

His first feeling was relief that he had been thrown almost on the very spot he had chosen to jump to before the train entered the tunnel. But this was succeeded by a stab of anguish from his back as he raised himself to his feet in the doorway of the Pullman. He put his hand behind his back and found first that his shirt had split all the way to his trousers. He allowed it to flow down his arms, and held it in one hand while he probed his back with the other.

"Ye gods," he murmured shakily, as he examined his hand after feeling his wound. "I must be bleeding like a stuck pig!"

Slowly he converted his shirt into a great bandage, wrapping it around his chest, under his armpits, and tying it below his chin, like a bra in reverse. While he was doing this, grunting as much from astonishment at his predicament as from pain, the express accelerated, and as it thundered along the decline his horror at this was added to the confusion of his feelings.

"I must stop this," he said thickly. "I must signal

the boy to cut the power off." He reeled into the Pullman. On the far side he seemed to remember there was a flat truck with nothing on it but a couple of logs. Perhaps if he got astride one of them he could make himself be seen.

From nowhere appeared the colossal torso of a man. It was white-coated, but the face was mottled, a sort of piebald, with only one deeply sunken eye, and the other the faintest smear at the point of the normal cheekbone.

"Get away! Get away!" screamed Coley, striking out at it wildly. One of the blows landed high on the man's chest. He teetered a moment and then, without bending, went over on his back. The material from which he was made was very light. He was no more than an amalgam of plastics and paint.

Coley looked down at the prostrate dummy and rubbed his bloodied hand over his forehead. "No sense in getting hysterical," he warned himself. He stepped over the prostrate figure, twisting to avoid the outstretched arm. He observed with revulsion that the fingers on the hand were webbed, a glittering duck-egg blue. Coley ran his tongue over his lips, tasting blood. "Take a brace," he admonished himself, reverting to the slang of his schooldays. "Don't let your imagination run away with you."

He staggered amongst the conclaves of seated gentlemen, forever impassive and at their ease in armchairs, content with the society in which they found themselves, unimpressed by the increasing momentum of the express, welded to their very chairs. Coley shot a glance over the gleaming carapace of one stern hock-drinker and out through the window. The variety of the landscape was flickering by with alarming speed, becoming a gale of altering colors. The coach was beginning to sway.

Coley broke into a run. The roar below him apprised him that the express was traveling over the suspension bridge. The bridge had been his pride, a labor of months, not bought whole, but built from wire and plywood in his leisure hours. He had no time now for gloating.

"I must get him to see me or I'm done for."

But beyond the Pullman he found another wagon, a restaurant car. In his haste he had forgotten that one. He dashed down the aisle, grabbing tables to steady himself against the rocking of the train as he went. They must be up to seventy now. Or rather about four miles an hour, he realized with bitterness.

Leaning a moment over one of the tables, he saw that the lamps in the center were bulky, heavy-looking objects. He heaved tentatively at one of them, and it snapped off at the base. The diners, with their hands in their laps, stared on across the table at each other, untroubled by the onslaught of this wild-eyed Englishman. The Englishman, naked to the waist, his shirt sleeves dangling red and filthy down his chest, his body flaming now with a dozen bruises, stood over them a second, clutching the lamp to him, panting heavily, then turned away and reeled on down the aisle. Down his retreating back the blood was flowing now freely. The shirt was inadequate to check it as it escaped from the savage wound he had sustained in the tunnel.

This time when he emerged at the doorway of the carriage he found himself looking at the open truck on which were chained four logs. He flung the lampstand ahead of him and it landed satisfyingly between two of the logs. He gathered his ebbing strength for the jump.

He was just able to make it. He caught his foot in one of the chains in mid-flight and crashed down on his face, but he saved himself from disaster by flinging one arm round a log. He sat up immediately and looked about him.

For a moment his vision was partly blocked as yet another train flashed by in the opposite direction. "Oh, God, what's he playing at?" whispered Coley. "He can't handle so many trains at once!"

The express was almost at the end of the long straight. It slowed for the curve right, at the bottom. For a brief time after that, it would be running directly under the control panel at which Brian was sitting. That would be his chance to make an impression. He hauled himself astride the top log and waited.

The express took the curve at a reduced pace, but squealing slightly nevertheless. Coley could sense most of the load concentrate on the inner wheels. Then he could see his son above him.

He waved frantically.

Brian seemed to rise slightly from his chair. His shadow leaped gigantically ahead of him, stretching forward and up on the slanting ceiling. Behind his head the glare of the Anglepoise lamp was almost unbearable. Coley was unable to make out the features of his son at all: there was only the silhouette. He couldn't tell if he had noticed anything.

With almost despairing violence he flung the lamp. He saw it speed in a low parabola out over the road which ran parallel to the track, bounce on the white space of Brian's shin exposed above his sock, and vanish in the darkness beyond. The enormous figure rose farther, towering now above the speeding express.

Coley was sure now that he had been seen. He made desperate motions with his hands, indicating that he would like a total shutdown of power. The boy waved. Coley turned sick. He stared down at his hands, pathetic little signals of distress. The probability was that the boy couldn't even see them.

But he should have been aware that something was wrong. Surely he must see that.

They tore through another station. They were taking the curves now at speed. They flashed across the scores of intersecting rails of the marshaling yard. The noise was like machine-gun fire. He saw another unit come into play; a two-car diesel slipped away south in a coquettish twinkle of chromium.

"He's showing off," thought Coley grimly. "He's going to try to bring every bloody train we've got into motion."

He knew now that the only way he could save himself would be somehow to get off the train. If only he didn't feel so hellishly bushed!

Coley was never tired. Other people seemed to be tired for him. In every project which he had ever undertaken, his adherents had flaked away at some stage, forgotten, like the jettisoned elements in a rocket flight. Hector Coley himself drove on to arrive at his object in perfect condition. But now he was tired, and he felt himself nearing exhaustion with his loss of blood and the battering he had taken.

There was just a chance, he thought, of a stop at Coleyville. The boy had evidently taken in the importance of that one. He'd postpone the final effort to get clear until Coleyville was reached.

He leaned over the cold metal of which the log was made, and embraced it like a lover. The metal was cold and refreshing against the skin of face and chest. Through his blurring vision he saw again the great gray plain, and the approaching scissors intersection before Coleyville. Once again the smart little roadster ground to a peremptory halt at the crossing. Other cars halted behind it.

But the express did not this time slacken speed. It went through Coleyville at sixty. For a fleeting instant he saw again the maroon face of the guard, the giant blond, the malevolence of the middle-aged schoolboy. Those waiting waited still. Those who had been waving waved on. Then Coleyville was gone, and the man on the log recognized that he would have to jump for it. He thought ahead.

Wistfully his mind passed over the swimming pool of the country club. If only that had been water! He winced at the appalling idea of crashing through glass.

But where else could he make it? Spring onto the

roof of the tunnel, as they entered? But no, the mountain above was too sheer; it would be like flinging himself against a brick wall. Then he remembered the trees which overhung the long straight beyond. He'd been in the Pullman last time they'd gone under those. But he might be able to grab one and hang from it long enough to let the express pass beneath him.

He fainted away.

When he came to, he found that the express was emerging from the tunnel. He wondered how many times he had made the circuit. Several times, probably. Looking across the countryside from this high vantage point he could see on almost every track trains and cars traveling, east, west, south, north.

He felt a cold wind blowing now powerfully across the track. It was horrendous, roaring. It threatened to drag his very hair out by the roots. The shirt sleeves were flapping like mad, trapped seagulls. He twisted his head to face the blast and looked on at the final horror.

His son had quitted the control panel. He was now squatting, setting a fan on the long gray meadow of carpet. In the whirlwind everything light in the lamdscape was going over, the waving figures of the yokels and children, the flimsier structures of paper cottages. The station at Coleyville was collapsing, while the people on the platform waited patiently.

Brian smiled. Coley saw him smile.

Then, as he thought that he must be obliged to relinquish his hold and be blown away to destruction, the boy picked the fan up again, and placed it where it always had been.

But he did not return to his seat at the control panel. He went out through the door and shut it behind him. The noise as it slammed was like a shell exploding.

The express went down the long straight through the suspension bridge and towards the curve at the bottom and reached a hundred miles an hour. Coley watched the overhanging branches of the trees sweep towards him. He climbed onto the logs and steadied himself with his feet braced against a knot to make this last leap. He realized that he would have to make it good the first time, and to hoist himself well clear of the onrushing roofs of following coaches.

Red, yellow, brown, green, the trees suddenly showed.

He made his effort.

He felt the spines run through his hands. Then the branch broke, and he was jammed in the doorway of the next carriage.

He pulled clear a spine which had remained in his flesh, and then lay there. He was broken. He waited for the express to derail.

But it did not derail. It swooped on the curve and screamed round it. Almost exuberantly it hurled itself at the next stretch running below the now abandoned control panel. Behind him he heard but did not see the last light trucks and petrol wagons go somersaulting off the track. For a moment there was a grinding check on the express: the wheels raced, then a link must have snapped and the wheels bit again. They surged forward.

The clatter as they started across the marshaling yard began again.

Coley got up quickly. The will which had devastated board rooms, concentrated now in his tiny figure, was the only part of him which had not been reduced to a scale of one in three hundred. He remembered that before getting onto the express at the outset of this misconceived adventure, he had sunk almost to his knees in the foam-rubber ballast on which the track was laid. In the marshaling yard there were acres of it! He stepped back on the log-bearing truck and looked quickly about him.

"Foam rubber," he said to himself, "not ballast."

He flung himself out, as if into a feather bed.

He lay for a moment luxuriously. He watched the express disappear in the direction of shattered Coleyville. He sighed. What a close thing!

Downstairs, Brian was buckling on his raincoat. His mother watched him anxiously.

"I think your father would prefer it if just this once more you helped him with his trains. It's a bit late to go out."

"No, he sent me away."

His mother sighed. She looked forward to an uncomfortable scene with Hector when he should deign to reappear. He probably wouldn't even eat his dinner and then be even more bad-tempered because he was hungry.

"Don't be long, then."

"I'm only going out to Billy's. We're going to

watch for a hedgehog he says comes out at night in his garden."

"All right then, but be sure to wrap up well."

Coley hauled himself to his feet. He stood alone, a figure of flesh and blood in a world of fakes.

"I shall never play with them again, not after this," he said quietly.

It was a decision, but it was accurate also as a prophecy. A sibilant hiss was all he heard of the diesel before it struck him. It was traveling at only three miles an hour, or call it sixty.

It killed him.

Before he died he thought: "How wretched to die here like this, tiny, probably not even found! They'll wonder whatever became of me."

He wished he might have been out altogether of the tiny world which had proved to be too big for him. It was his dying wish.

No one doubted that it had been murder when Hector Coley was found stretched out across the toy world which had been his great hobby and pride. But so battered and bloodied and broken a figure could only have resulted from the attack of a maniac of prodigious strength.

"He was still playing with the models when he was surprised," reported the Inspector. "The current was on, and about ten of them had come to rest against his body. To be frank, though, he looked as if about ten real ones had hit him."

The Pram

A. W. Bennett

Chorn was a man full of meanness and all unchar-
itableness. He didn't want the job of burying Old
Sam at all; he'd have settled for dumping him in a
ditch. But he wanted the one thing—the fifty-pound
fee—and Sam had made it very awkward for him,
dying in such a public, heroic, dramatic fashion and
leaving a will making Chorn responsible for the
burial.

Of course, that was Chorn's profession. Funeral
undertaker. Burials. Not cremations; he hated them.
Had a thing about them. He advertised as such in
the local paper. Apart from that, he'd never had
anything to do with Old Sam, always shooed him
off his doorstep. Lots wouldn't have anything to
do with Sam. He wasn't the most salubrious person
in the town, with his pram, his ragged clothes,

tattered trilby, beard, oversize shoes. "Beaver," the kiddies called after him.

That pram had seen life—and death. It had carried lively, lovely kiddies, scrap metal, a gramophone, fruit, manure, firewood, and a corpse—Barmey Betty. In fact, Barmey Betty had her last, and probably only, ride in that pram. To Chorn's funeral parlor, Old Sam pushing her there.

Betty left four pounds—tucked into her stocking—when she died. Chorn wouldn't do anything with her for that. Old Sam somehow gathered together another twenty-one pounds, and Chorn agreed to tuck her under for that, provided Sam delivered the cadaver to his parlor.

So she arrived in the pram. It was a conglomeration of a dozen previous prams. When a wheel fell off or crumpled, Sam begged, borrowed, or scrounged another. Same with body or handles. Or somebody gave him one. Many people had a soft spot for the old man—a bit simple he might be, but no harm in him; do a good turn for anybody. Same went for Barmey Betty. Either or both would do a bit of gardening for whatever the customer could afford—often for nothing, if the truth be told—for not everybody always plays fair with simple people who don't know a hayseed from a cannonball.

Betty would do washing in people's own homes, go errands, carry coals, baby-sit (wonderfully good with children she was), scrape potatoes—and always push the old pram if Sam wasn't using it.

Sam would clean cars, lay crazy paving, trim hedges, sharpen scissors and shears, fix mowers—

and always push the pram if Betty wasn't using it.

Nobody knew how they'd come together. They
were already full of years when they joined forces.
"Much too old for marrying," Betty said. "Sam's
old shed collapsed, so I took him into my house.
Makes for company."

Betty's "house" was one room. It had been the
brewhouse at the back of a house. When this house
was condemned and demolished, the brewhouse
for some reason was left standing, and Barmey Betty
took possession.

Ages ago Betty wheeled an old gramophone round
in the pram, stopped here and there to play a few
tunes and collect—maybe—a few coins, then plod-
ded on. Transistors finished that effort. She wheeled
round firewood and clothes pegs. Sam collected
scrap metal; delivered manure and spuds. The lovely
kiddies? That's Betty's tale. She told how she en-
joyed pushing lovely kiddies in the pram when it
was new. Betty's? Who knows?

Then she died suddenly. Heart failure, the medic
said. She'd pushed an old mangle, heavy, uphill to
the scrap merchant. That night she lay resting in
her "house" with Old Sam watching beside her.

"She just give a sigh and left me like a light," he
told Chorn. "She told me to look after the old pram.
Precious it was to her; held some lovely nippers
once. Said I should burn it when I died. She wants
the ashes on our grave. Worries me that: burn it
when I die. Not before I die, but when. Takes some
thinking about, dunnit?"

Chorn hadn't time to listen to his meanderings. "Take your heartbreakings somewhere else. What sorrowings do you expect from me for twenty-five pounds? The coffin cost that."

Old Sam reckoned he could have knocked a better coffin up from old planks for maybe a quid; but it's no use arguing with an undertaker who's got the body of your old mate.

Sam wouldn't hear of a pauper's grave. "I miss her every morning and every evening and every waking hour of the day," he said to me.

He was the only follower. He didn't listen much to the minister; just whispered something down to the coffin, turned away, wiped wet eyes on battered trilby, and shambled away.

He worked all the hours of daylight after that. "Got to save fifty at least for when I die," he explained to me. "Got to have enough for me *and* the old pram to be burned and the ashes scattered on our grave. I'm responsible to Betty for that, gave her my oath. Pram sacred to her. Carried lovely babies once. Can't be left in this cold, harsh world. She believed that something of those babies—souls, perhaps—lingered on, still clung to the pram. When I go the pram must burn—worries me, puzzles me, that. When I go; not before or after. When! How will I hang on?"

Perhaps he was worrying about that when he died? For he did a daft thing: walked into a flooded river, although he couldn't swim a stroke. I prefer to assume that he was thinking about those lovely babies—for it was a lovely baby he followed into the river. The toddler tripped, fell in, and the current was carrying her away when Old Sam ran in—yes, ran in. I'd never seen him run before. Miraculously he seemed to run on top of the water—remember, our Lord walked on the waters—until he caught hold of the toddler. Then he sank. If I've got to give any explanation, I'd say the size of his boots—some big fellow's castoffs—had something to do with it; gave him some "lift." Then they filled with water, and so did he.

I'm glad I saw him from the bridge where I was patroling. I'm a copper or was then. Sergeant now. The current was sweeping Sam and the kiddie towards me. I slipped off tunic and shoes and went in. Oh, I'm no hero. I can swim like a fish, always could. Anyway, part of a copper's job. It wasn't part of Sam's job—and he swam like a brick.

I got them out. Got a commendation. Sam got pneumonia. The kid got a telling off from her mother.

Sam died. A solicitor said he'd left thirty-nine pounds, but the kid's dad made it up to the fifty pounds the will talked about. The reporters made a fuss about the rescue, insisted Chorn put on a good show. They could have started a subscription if they'd wanted. Chorn asked them to, but they refused, for they knew Chorn would have commandeered all they collected and still only made a skimpy job of the funeral. He was the meanest devil in the town—nobody would have gone to him if there was another undertaker anywhere near. We all have to die sometime, so Chorn prospered.

Only a few attended Sam's funeral, but that was

more than would have been there but for the sacrificial manner of his death. He was lowered into the same grave as Betty, and some say they heard a distinct sigh from one or other of them, but then, I always say people are fanciful at funerals. Chorn didn't burn the old pram on his grave there and then. Said he'd keep it in his warehouse and burn it later. A huge warehouse he had, full of expensive timber, and bronzes for coffin decorating.

Some people don't place much importance on a simple ceremony—like getting married. Sam and Betty didn't. But burning the pram and having the ashes on their grave meant everything to them. The pram had been the center of their lives. I never did trust Chorn. I found out a few weeks later that he'd sold that pram for ten shillings. I made him buy it back; told him he'd have to do as the will said. It was part of the contract he'd made when he accepted the fifty pounds.

He said he'd do it after a decent interval. Weeks went by.

"Why wait?" I asked him. "Maybe Betty and Sam are waiting for it in the better world."

"A sentimental cop," he sneered. "I'll see to it in my own good time."

Then one of the gravediggers noticed that Barmey Betty's/Old Sam's grave was disturbed. He leveled it. Two mornings later he found the surface disturbed again; leveled it again.

"Them two is disturbed about the pram," he surmised.

Surface disturbed again. "Colliery subsidence. Old

workings collapsing down below," the Borough Engineer explained in a superior fashion.

"Ain't no pits ever been round the cemetery," commented every old stager within miles.

"Dogs playing about, then," the Engineer insisted, not to be beaten.

"Why pick on that one grave?" asked the gravedigger.

"I suppose you think Old Sam is turning over and over down there?" asked the Surveyor sarcastically.

"Him or Barmey Betty," answered the digger seriously. "They'll come up and see Chorn off if he don't do something soon. They want to get the feel of those ashes on them."

They leveled the grave out again and things went quiet for a while. Then when I was on night duty I saw a wonderful sight. Chorn's warehouse doors slowly slid open; there was a clammy draft and a sudden waft and out came the old pram and set off—uphill. Nobody pushing it, nobody with it. The night was dark. The only sound, a slight squeak from the doors—Chorn was too mean to provide oil.

I suppose what I should have done was close the doors and notify my Inspector. I was so flabbergasted that I forgot about the doors and simply followed the pram—open-mouthed. There was a tenseness in the atmosphere that set my nerves aquiver.

I couldn't arrest the pram. I tried to stop it, but couldn't bear my hands on the handle. Too cold.

Cold beyond belief. Deadly, icy cold. The very air at that end of the pram was too cold to breathe. It was a warm night but my breath steamed when I was at that end. I hurried to the front and tried to bar the way but the pram swung round and the cold end rammed me and I jumped a foot. Supernaturally cold; it would be death to linger at that end for long—but someone was pulling it now—some *thing* was.

The only sound was the soft thud-thud of muffled footsteps. I'd heard them before. Old Sam's. He often tied his oversize shoes with rags or rope, for he wore them until they were literally falling apart. It was the first deep hour of the dark—the hour of magic and mystery.

"Sam—Sam, are you there?" I whispered, glad the Inspector couldn't hear me.

No answer, although I could hear Sam's feet only feet from me.

"What are you up to, Sam?" I called, a little louder. I'm a down-to-earth man, and this is a go-ahead world, but all sorts of things from the dim and distant past still linger on. It pays to be careful when you're tampering with unknown powers. Was that a sigh from Sam, or a wandering breeze? No leaves stirred.

"Taking this to the cemetery?" I asked foolishly, for he'd reached the open gates—at least the pram had. But something was different. Then I realized there were no night sounds: no hum of insects, no nocturnal adventuring in the undergrowth. The creatures of the night had fled—from something beyond their understanding, something not of this world.

The new moon peeped out from behind a drifting cloud bank. Just the pram, teetering along the rough path, unaided, unaccompanied. I groaned inwardly. What a setup for a common-or-garden copper! I hurried forward, suddenly determined to stop that pram at all cost. We couldn't have a disturbance amongst the hallowed graves of the long-dead—even by the half-dead.

What had Sam said? Something about burning the pram when he died; not before or after, but then. Perhaps he wasn't fully dead yet, as the dead reckon. Half-dead; some duty yet to perform before he goes to eternal rest. Betty couldn't be doing this, however barmey; she was below him!

I grabbed the handles and my hands froze to them. Whatever and whoever this elemental creature was, he couldn't have come from the hot regions. I wrenched my hands away painfully, yelped as I left some skin behind—and I distinctly heard a throaty chuckle.

The pram rocked on, straight to their grave. There was a long hollow in the center. The pram climbed astride, straddled the grave. I heard a rasping sound, a small flame appeared. Had a wheel scraped a stone or had something struck a match? By its light I saw a heap of rags in the pram; a moment later they burst into flame. Evidently the heavy body of the pram was made of wood, dry, for soon it was a mass of flames.

Suddenly a shower of sparks flew past me, making me duck—yet there was not a breath of wind. I turned to watch the comet and tail; it flew as if to a definite target, somewhere in the town. The pram framework buckled until there was merely a heap of twisted metal on the grave—and ashes. I bent to lift off the metal; it seemed sacrilege to leave it there. They—Sam and Betty—had wanted the *ashes* of the pram.

A sudden sharp cry of warning and I was pushed smartly backwards. The buckled metal levitated, was dropped on to a piece of waste ground near— and the grass sizzled. Sam had saved me from a nasty burn.

Nobody had seen the blaze apparently. I was alone in a deserted graveyard. Yes, alone, quite alone—for I felt the "presence" fade away. I shone my torch; the hollow in the grave was slowly filling—and absorbing the ashes. The ashes of their precious pram were joining Sam and Betty. Peace almost audibly descended upon them. I bared my head.

Greater love hath no ghost than this, that he give up his eternal repose for another—as it seemed that Sam had done for Betty.

"I'm glad you got back okay, Sam," I murmured and turned towards the town; and saw another fire!

Chorn's warehouse. His valuable timber.

I remembered the sparks rushing past me.

I knew Chorn wasn't insured. "Waste of money," he'd said. "I'm far too careful to ever have a fire."

Now, he'd got one. Sam the instigator? We could never charge him with it.

They say there's a good woman behind every man. Had Barmey Betty given him a shove-up? From the grave? Life is full of surprises. We'll never know.

When I arrived at the fiercely burning warehouse the fire chief told me that Chorn, mad with rage and dismay, had evaded the firemen and rushed in, trying to save his property. The flames had engulfed him.

"The undertaker has been cremated," he said simply.

Next day they found his calcined bones, crushed when the roof fell in.

In the daylight they looked just like the pram ashes had looked last night.

Mr. Ash's Studio

H. Russell Wakefield

It was the return of the road-breaking battalion with their accursed compressed-air drills which made Mr. Horrocks' graying hairs bristle with determination. He could oathfully endure the foul orchestra of horns and gears, the cacophony of canned dance music, even the piano-pounding of the infernal brat in the flat below. But at the first renewal of that quivering, booming patter from East Street he knew something must be done if he was to finish his novel.

"Why not take a studio while you're looking for another flat?" said a friend in the club. He picked up a copy of the *Connoisseur*. "Here you are . . . 'Within ten minutes' walk of Knightsbridge Tube Station, roomy, outdoor studio. Very quiet. Easy terms.' Why not have a look at that? There are heaps of others vacant if it doesn't suit you."

Very occasionally, about twice a year, Mr. Horrocks acted with extreme decision. Within ten minutes he was on his way to the agent's. He was a small, sturdy, thrusting little person of forty-six. He had a long head, rather flat along the top, the hair at the sides brushed forward, which gave him a slightly old-fashioned appearance. His eyes were very quick and dark, mouth small and mobile, chin pointed but emphatic.

He made a rather contradictory impression on the discerning beholder, alert but contemplative, irascible but benign. He regarded censors, kill-joys, puritans and that sort with an unbridled loathing in theory—but if he came in actual contact with one of them he was in practice courteous, understanding, reasonable, inquisitive; the true novelist's mind being inevitably timeserving.

"Anyone in Rooper's Court will direct you," said the agent, handing him a key. "Ask for Mr. Ash's studio."

"Thank you," replied Mr. Horrocks and trotted off. Keeping a wary eye open, he eventually discovered Rooper's Court, which began in a narrow arched passageway off the Brompton Road and developed into what had been known in his youth as a "Mews." Now it was a series of lockup garages and an occasional small private house—rebuilt coachmen's quarters. There were many chauffeurs sluicing and attending to their charges.

Mr. Horrocks, looking round for a guide, caught sight of a tall young man standing at the door of a charming little yellow house with gay blue window boxes. Mr. Horrocks went up to him and put his question.

"Certainly," he replied in a pleasant, genial way. "Come with me." He conducted Mr. Horrocks to an opening on the right-hand side round a corner where there was a small railed-in grass space. At the far end was a rather high hut with a corrugated-iron roof, over which leaned a plane tree with many drooping branches.

"That's the studio," said the tall young man. "The door is up at the other end."

"Thanks very much," said Mr. Horrocks. "It looks nice and quiet."

The young man seemed to be considering something. "Are you a painter?" he asked presently.

"No," replied Mr. Horrocks. "I try to write. My name is Samuel Horrocks; but I don't suppose you've ever heard of it."

"Of course I have. And may I say I greatly admire your stories of the supernatural. May I ask how you were put on to this studio?"

"Oh, I just happened to see it advertised."

The young man remained thoughtful for a moment. Then he appeared to make up his mind. "Well," he said, "I hope you'll find it all right for your purposes. My name is Landen and I live in that little yellow house. If I can be of any service to you, let me know." Mr. Horrocks thanked him and they said good-by.

"Very courteous young fellow," thought Mr. Horrocks as he stepped forward. "Looks highly intelligent, too, but I wonder what service he thought he could render me?" Ah, there was the door. He pushed the key in the lock. He had to use some force to open the door as it was jammed from damp, he supposed, at the bottom and sides.

He found himself in a room surprisingly more spacious than its exterior suggested. There appeared to be two rooms, as a matter of fact, for there was another door at the far end. The place was lit by three high windows. It smelled rather fusty and there were patches of damp on the distempered walls. Ah, there was an easel with a picture on it and a couple of rather dilapidated chairs.

He'd see what was behind the other door. It *was* another room, quite a small one, full of odds and ends, packing cases, an oil stove, a kettle and so on. What a peculiar smell! What was that red stain on the small packing case? He bent down. Good heavens, it was alive, a cluster of moths. How very curious! Beautiful color. They must be feeding on something. He put out his hand to disturb them when suddenly they all sprang up at his face. Little brutes! He lashed out at them and beat a hasty retreat, shutting the door behind him. Venomous little beasts!

Well, what about this studio? He wasn't greatly taken with it, but it was most certainly quiet. Mr. Horrocks was a shop assistant's glad-dream, for he almost invariably took the first thing offered him and hurried out of the shop. The last thing he wanted was to go hunting about, fussing with agents and keys and asking his way and that sort of thing. He wanted a place to work in and he wanted it at once.

This would surely do. Not in the winter, perhaps, but with the summer coming on—

Why not in the winter? Mr. Horrocks vaguely considered this proviso. Too damp, perhaps, and also—well, there was something rather—rather somber about it. It was the contrast, no doubt, between its aloofness, quietness and isolation and the raging stress and promiscuous din only a hundred yards away. Something like that. Oh, yes, it would do. He'd get a desk in and a stove for the damp, and just exploit that aloofness and quiet. That was settled.

He strolled over to the easel. Portrait of a woman. Good-looking girl—in a way very beautiful, and yet there was something about her expression—something enigmatic. Wonder who this fellow Ash was. Ah, there were his palette and brushes on the floor behind the easel. Curious smudged, rainbow thing, a palette. It was rather humiliating, but he hadn't really the smallest knowledge of the way a painter went to work. However, he'd never pretended otherwise.

How loud his footsteps sounded on the wood floor! Showed how quiet it was. Before leaving he peeped through the door into the small room. Yes, there they were back again, forming a sort of pattern—wonderful patch of color, dark ruby. Little brutes seemed to be staring at him. He laughed out loud. What an echo! He must get some lunch. He'd take the studio that afternoon for a month. That was settled and a great relief.

As he caught hold of the door on getting outside,

it seemed to swing hard at him of its own momentum and it slammed harshly, thrusting him back. He was a little ruffled. Not exactly a hospitable atmosphere about that place, he thought.

The tall young man was still standing outside the yellow house as he repassed up the court. "Well?" he asked.

"I've decided to take it," said Mr. Horrocks. "It's not, perhaps, a very cheerful spot, but its quietness decided me."

The young man nodded. "Are you taking it for long?"

"No, just by the month."

"I see. Well, good luck with the book—I hope you'll give us some more ghost stories soon."

"It's rather difficult to get plots for them," replied Mr. Horrocks, "but I'll do my best. Good morning."

Three days later he revisited the studio, which now housed a desk, a couple of comfortable chairs and his portable typewriter. It was a brilliantly fine May morning and the place seemed a bit more genial, but not really very much, he considered. However, now for work. He was about a third of the way through his novel and irritatingly uncertain exactly how to develop it. Also he had promised his agent to have a ghost story ready fairly soon for the Christmas number of a magazine which paid very well. But at the moment he hadn't an idea in his head. For the time being he would concentrate on the novel. He sat down at his desk and began to cogitate.

His weakness, he knew it well, was a tendency

to flippancy. The more he saw and read of the world and its denizens, the harder he found it to take them with the proper seriousness. As far as the tale of humanity was concerned he was inclined to laugh at the wrong places, a serious flaw in a novelist! His characters would adopt an unbecoming impishness at critical moments and mock their creator's efforts to control them. It was probably due to the fact that their creator had never succeeded in measuring humanity flatteringly in accordance with the cosmic scale. He was, therefore, delighted to find that the atmosphere of Mr. Ash's studio was an excellent corrective to this levity. He wrote a whole chapter by lunchtime, a very critical chapter, and he knew that it was good. The motley streak was rigidly eliminated from it.

With an aching arm but satisfied soul he got up at half-past one, yawned, stretched himself and found himself regarding the picture on the easel. Seen by this stronger light it appeared a very vivid piece of work. It almost seemed as if it had been more worked on than when he'd seen it before. Certainly her face was a puzzle. He went up to it and covered first her eyes, then her mouth and chin with his hand in an attempt to discover where the secret of that oddness lay. As a result he decided it was immanent and not to be traced.

He'd have a look and see what those little red devils were doing. There they were bunched on the packing case making that same pattern, motionless and intent. Funny pattern, almost like a human face. Vague memories of "bug-hunting" at school came back to him. He was very certain that nothing resembling them had ever found its way into his killing bottle. Singular markings on their heads. He bent down, and at once the swarm rose together and flew savagely into his face. He struck out at them. How extraordinary, it seemed impossible to touch one! Artful little dodgers. What a filthy smell they made, nauseating and corrupt. He'd leave them alone in future.

He spent the afternoon at Kew Gardens, in his opinion the most delectable place in the world on a fine spring day. As he strolled about the lawns and threw crumbs to the birds, he sought some inspiration for that infernal ghost story. A reviewer had once credited him with the possession of a "malignant imagination" for such fiction. At the moment he had a malignant lack of it. All the same the atmosphere of that studio ought to be kinetic.

Presently he felt like a rest and sat down on a seat by the rhododendrons. Drowsily he began to daydream. A succession of images elusively patrolled his brain. A girl's head on an easel—a dark stain on a packing case. He found himself examining the studio almost inch by inch, for his visualizing power was very highly developed. He scrutinized the girl's face closely, and then was jerked back into full consciousness, for it had seemed to him that a brush had fallen on the face and slightly emphasized the line from her left nostril to upper lip. Amusing illusion! Might be an idea for a story there; whole thing taking place in narrator's subconscious. Damned difficult. Well, he must be getting home; those road-breakers would have knocked off by the time he reached there.

From then on he went to the studio four days a week, always in the morning, sometimes in the afternoon. He invariably approached it with oddly mixed emotions. Never had he known any place more stimulating to his imagination, yet he never felt at home there. The moment he unlocked the door he felt a sense of obscure excitement which, in fact, began to come over him as soon as he passed into Rooper's Court, and intensified itself until he was actually inside and face to face with the girl on the easel. And as he wrote he often paused and looked up at her.

Each time he came to the studio she seemed subtly and indefinably to have changed, developed, become at once more "realized" yet harder to nail down and analyze. He imagined that was what was meant by learning to "see" a painting; that like a poem or a piece of music it only revealed its inner, profounder meaning to those who lavished as much care on deciphering it as the artist had in inscribing it. She was very useful, too, for she seemed to have become identified in a way with the chief female character in his novel—"heroine" would have been a somewhat satirical term for that dark-hearted vampire.

And how excellently and reassuringly the book was going! For once his publisher's plaintive and oft-repeated blurbed insistence that "Samuel Horrocks' latest work is also his greatest" showed every evidence of being justified. Certainly it revealed an almost ruthless lack of flippancy. As it moved to its inevitable climax the shadows darkened and gathered round it. That meant drastically revising the first third of it, a laborious necessity but unescapable.

He left the little room and the moths alone. Their business was none of his, he felt, and somehow they were peculiar to the place. He gathered that Mr. Ash, whoever he might be, had felt a keen interest in them, for he discovered a sketchbook of his, presumably his, on one of the window ledges. This contained dozens of preliminary studies for the girl's head, each one decoratively framed in moth clusters.

One of them gave him rather a dubious reaction, for the girl's head was flung hard back from her shoulders and there was poured over her face a stream of dark red, delicately though unmistakably articulated into the couched shape of moths. What the artist was thinking about when he put his pencil to work on so morbid a conception Mr. Horrocks was at a loss to understand; yet it fascinated him, and he several times examined it in a hurried, shamefaced way. All the same, if it hadn't been someone else's property he was almost certain he would have torn it into very small pieces.

He spent, perhaps, twenty hours a week in the studio, yet in a sense he was there for much longer. That was due to his recently developed tendency to daydream, reinforced by his abnormal power of visualization. This tendency was by no means welcome; in fact it was decidedly exasperating, for his subconscious, the breeding ground, he supposed, of these daydreams, appeared to be quite determined that he should be compelled to take an urgent interest in what occurred at the studio when its tenant wasn't there. Of course *nothing* went on, and yet the fact remained that he might be taking a walk or trying to read when all of a sudden he would find himself, as *it* were, just inside the studio and regarding its interior.

His view of it was hazy and it appeared much diminished, but it was quite recognizable. He couldn't see his desk or chairs, but there was the girl's head on the easel, and there were the windows and the door into the little room. And he was forced to admit there was frequently something else, *someone* to be more precise, and that he—yes, it was a man—was moving about. A tall man with an odd walk, as if he limped. But, however hard he concentrated, he could never quite get this person into focus. The effort to do so often made him sweat and his heart race, but he simply couldn't get a proper look at this person's face. Surely he was tall and dark. Who could he be?

While he was still in this fussed state and before he pulled himself together and called himself a fool, he often felt a violent, crazy impulse to dash off to Rooper's Court to make quite certain whether there was or was not someone prowling about the studio. More than once he could only just rally enough strength of mind to resist this insensate craving.

He reassured himself that his eccentric preoccupation with a dingy hut was a symptom of over-work—not exactly that, perhaps, but excessive absorption in his novel. But how blessed that all those wavering uncertain currents had coalesced so perfectly into a steady stream. He had to thank the dingy hut for that, and he could see the end in sight.

He met Landen when he was leaving the studio late one afternoon and accepted his invitation to come in for a glass of sherry. The little yellow house was as charming inside as out, fitted and furnished with a nice careless discretion.

"So you really find the place a congenial work-shop?" his host inquired on hearing of the progress the book was making.

"Well, it depends on what you mean by that," replied Mr. Horrocks. "I've certainly written forty thousand words there and, as golfers say, I 'don't want them back.' But congenial—well, I mustn't be ungrateful—but it's not an adjective I feel appropriate to the place."

Landen was silent for a moment. "No," he said presently, "I think I understand what you mean."

"You've been inside it?"

"Oh, yes," said Landen.

"It's got an atmosphere of its own. Almost, one might say, a personality. There are places like that, I think."

"Are you clairvoyant in that way? I mean have you had actual experiences of a psychic sort?"

"As a matter of fact, I have," replied Mr. Horrocks, "quite a number. But as I've found these experiences were not shared by others, I've kept quiet about them."

"That is my case, also," said Landen, "and I've learned to keep my mouth shut, when to open it results in being regarded as a self-assertive liar. It must be a great relief to you to get them out of your system in the form of fiction. Are you writing a story now?"

Mr. Horrocks shrugged his shoulders. "I'm not sure," he said, "but I'm inclined to think there *is* one forming itself in my harassed old pate. But I mustn't hurry it or keep pulling it up to have a look, like an impatient fisherman. If it's hooking something I shall feel that unmistakable 'bite' when the time comes."

"That's rather a revealing metaphor," said Landen. "I can't write fiction—'think of stories'—myself. I'm an architect, but I understand just what you mean. By the way, I always remember that story of yours, *At the Going Down of the Sun;* I believe the Ray theory of psychic phenomena you hinted at there is the most probable."

"It was the undoubted evidence for phantoms of the living which gave me the idea," replied Mr. Horrocks, somewhat gratified.

"Yes, quite," said Landen. "By the way, you don't work at night in the studio, do you?"

"I haven't so far."

"Well, I shouldn't. There are some tough characters about this neighborhood at night. If they saw a light they might pay you a somewhat unceremonious visit."

"I should, of course, lock the door," said Mr. Horrocks.

"Yes, naturally, but all the same, I shouldn't run any risk."

At length the day came when Mr. Horrocks typed the word "Finis" and the date below it, May 29th, and knew that the preceding ninety thousand words represented the best work he'd done in his life; so good and yet so alien to his customary manner both in atmosphere and style that he hardly recognized it as his. Almost, he modestly said to himself, as if he'd been a tiny bit inspired. Tomorrow he'd hand it to his publisher and go straight off to Cornwall for a long rest. And then he'd start hunting for a tolerably quiet flat. So it was good-by to the studio.

Would he be sorry to bid it farewell? Once again he failed to give a decided answer to that question. It had been a most excellent tonic and stimulant to his imagination, yet he *was* a little afraid of it. Yes, better to say the word, there was something about it which ruffled his nerves and, no doubt, caused that ridiculous yet oppressive daydreaming. He'd have a last leisurely stroll round it; and a last look at the girl.

It really was a most baffling illusion for he could have sworn that the expression on her face had drastically changed. She was still exquisitely beautiful and she'd always look like one to be wary of, but now she wore an air of mocking, heartless frigidity, a most lovely, perilous vampire, a devil. He had a sudden desire to crash his fist into her face.

And then he laughed at himself and said out loud, "Well, my most adorable but evil one, I shan't see you again. Give my love to Mr. Ash and—" He stopped abruptly. He had spoken in a light, bantering tone, but the echo of his words came back to him in a most mournful yet somehow mocking way. He felt a sudden gust of uneasiness and depression and impulsively turned the canvas round. On the back of it he casually noticed some carefully drawn but undecipherable hieroglyphics.

And now for a last look at the little red beasts. Yes, there they were, glowing, motionless and obscene, like a stain of blood with a hundred eyes. Supposing he picked up that piece of planking and crashed it down on them. The little devils seemed to read his thoughts, for they sprang up at him and drove him from the room. How they stank! Well, that was that. As he opened the door to leave he took a last look back and then the door swung hard at him—runk!—and slammed to.

As he strolled towards his club for lunch his mind turned to the subject of that infernal ghost story he'd got to write. It was beginning to get urgent. Obscurely he felt that the studio was the only possible place in which to conceive of it and write it. Perhaps he'd given it up too soon. What a curse it was! Just as he'd finished a most delicate and exhausting piece of work, he'd got to tackle another. Well, he would have *one* day off, he told himself irritably. If his imagination wouldn't let him rest, he'd drown it.

The bank rate had been lowered that morning

and his business friends at the club, who'd been feeling the overdraft severely, were in the mood for some alcoholic enthusiasm and celebration. Mr. Horrocks was reasonably abstemious, but for once he found their spiritual state catching and comforting. Consequently, after a large and cheerful lunch, sherry, hock and a double port, he was more than prepared for a restorative snooze in his favorite chair in the chess room. It was sweet and dreamless, so he was all the more annoyed when, on waking, he found himself staring, not at the trees in St. James's Park, but straight down the length of the studio. And there was that—no, he *wouldn't* look! He got up brusquely and went to the bar.

He completely mistrusted the *fata Morgana* amenities of alcohol, but his nerves were jangled and something must be done. He did it with discretion. The result was quite unexpected and bizarre, for he began to experience an exalted resolve to visit the studio again that night, and then and there conceive of that accursed short story. He was sure of it. He'd have a good dinner, just enough to keep his optimism untarnished but leave his head fairly clear, and *he'd get that story*. It sounded ludicrous, but he'd had such irrational surges of certainty before and they'd always been justified. He *would* go.

Successfully maintaining his resolution and good hope, he hailed a taxi at ten-thirty and twenty minutes later was at Rooper's Court, feeling rather excited and venturous. Yet the enterprise began to reveal itself rather more starkly in the court than it had in the club smoking room. It was a boisterous night, the wind veering to the west and stiffening sharply. The weather was breaking, and with much low cloud it was very dark. Rooper's Court appeared desolate and uninviting. Landen seemed to be in, as there was a light in his sitting room. This reminded Mr. Horrocks of his advice about not visiting the studio after dark. Oh, well, he could take care of himself.

As he turned the corner he took an electric torch from his pocket. That tree made it damned dark. What a wind! Curious sound the branches made on the roof; like stealthy footsteps. Ah, there was the keyhole. Door had stuck as usual. He put his shoulder to it, whereupon it yielded so suddenly that he staggered forward and dropped the torch. Then the door swung back and crashed. Now where was that cursed torch? His hands swept the floor. Ah, there it was. Click. Click. Blast the thing, it wouldn't work now! Yes, just a faint glow. He'd wait a moment till his eyes got used to it.

Rather a fool to have come. What was he really doing in this rather dreadful place? How those branches lashed the roof. Yes, really rather a dreadful place. What would those moths be doing? Probably just making that pattern and listening to him, their foul little eyes staring and intent. He moved forward cautiously. He could just see his way now. What a daunting suggestion of menace seemed hovering in the place. Well, that was an absurd exaggeration. After all, that was the atmosphere he'd come to absorb.

Hullo! What was that? It almost seemed as if the room had become smaller, as if the walls had come crouching in towards him. Ah, there was the easel! But he'd turned the girl's face round! Who could have—good God, the moths were on it! He stood motionless and rigid, his heart beating wildly, for wasn't her head flung back from the shoulders and weren't they crawling, crawling—! And weren't those walls closing in on him, and who was that standing and watching him from the small door?

For a moment he felt he could never move again; then he wrenched himself free and began to run for the door. He dropped the torch and with trembling hands groped his way along a wall. Where was the door! Was that it? No! Yes! As he flung it open it seemed as though myriad little wings came beating round his eyes. He tore down the path, the door crashing to behind him.

As he reached the corner someone approached him. He flinched back. Then a voice said: "It's all right. This is Landen. You're perfectly safe. Come with me—"

"But how did you know?" cried Mr. Horrocks hysterically.

"I heard you shouting," he replied quietly, "and guessed the rest."

Mr. Horrocks walked panting by his side to his house and into the sitting room. There was a tantalus and glasses on the table. "Sit down," said Landen, "and make yourself comfortable while I mix you a drink."

"It's very good of you," said Mr. Horrocks. "I'm

afraid I quite lost my head, but I had rather a shock. I see now I should have taken your advice, but I didn't realize—"

"Perhaps I should have been more explicit," replied Landen, handing him a glass, "but as you found the place congenial for your writing I didn't want to prejudice you against it. But it is, of course, well, shall we say, highly impregnated. You've gone into such matters far more than I, but as you have stated, they remain without convincing explanation."

"Absolutely so," replied Mr. Horrocks, raising his glass with a still unsteady hand. "Any tentative suggestions I have made were simply guesswork. There is no theory ever advanced which begins to cover the ground. It was horrible, horrible!"

"I'll give you such facts as I know about that studio," said Landen, sitting down and lighting a cigarette. "It was built by a person named Raphael Ash four years ago. His father was a Highland Scot in business at Teheran. There he married a Persian woman of high degree. Their son was brought up in Persia and eventually sent to Oxford. A friend of mine was up at New College with him. He was a very enigmatic character—outwardly imperturbable and bland, yet keeping himself aloof from college life and somehow forbidding.

"He was extremely unpopular for some reason, I believe, not unconnected with a certain doubt as to how he spent his plentiful leisure time. The occupants of the other rooms in his corridor thought at times they saw and heard dubious things. So four enterprising and intoxicated sportsmen broke into his rooms one night. They got rather badly frightened, but would say nothing of their experiences. By a coincidence they all died within a year or so.

"Ash came under the notice of the college authorities and was sent down after a couple of terms, for reasons best known to themselves. Whereupon he built this studio and began to paint. He also fell in love. I may say he inherited a great deal of money. The lady concerned seemed for a time to reciprocate his feelings and she certainly made his money fly. However, someone else desired her and he was just as rich and socially far more eligible. I knew this lady and you have seen a brilliantly clever likeness of her, but no portrait could do her justice. She was exquisitely lovely, an accomplished actress and an utterly amoral, soulless rogue.

"Well, she married the other man and went to live with him at his place in Surrey. A few weeks later she met her death. She was seen one afternoon by a gamekeeper running through a wood near the house. He stated at the inquest that she was beating out at something with her hands. He imagined she was being attacked by a swarm of bees and ran after her; but before he could reach her she had fallen over the edge of a quarry. She was dying when he got to her, but still beating out with her hands as if to keep something from her face. Shortly after, Ash was shot dead in the small room in the studio."

"Good God!" exclaimed Mr. Horrocks. "Was it suicide?"

"That was the verdict," replied Landen slowly. "The evidence was slightly conflicting. One witness stated that he had heard voices coming from the studio that afternoon, and the medical evidence was slightly indefinite. However, the coroner was satisfied. Well, that's all I know about Mr. Ash and his studio—or almost. When I came to live here I discovered it had a certain reputation amongst the frequenters of the court. I wondered why, got the key and went there late one winter evening. And then I no longer wondered. It has had one temporary tenant besides you since Ash died. He gave it up after a few days. I believe it is to be pulled down soon. And now you must have another little drink and I'll join you."

"Well, just a very small one. There is one other thing; those moths—"

"You will not find their like in the Natural History Museum," replied Landen. "Perhaps you might search the world over and never do so; for I once described them to a distinguished Orientalist and he told me that he had never met anyone who had encountered such an insect, but that he'd received obscure hints concerning such creatures, though there was a very general reluctance to refer to them. Once or twice he had succeeded in overcoming this reluctance. He gathered that they were known as 'The Servants of Eblis'—in a rough translation. Personally he didn't believe in their existence and was greatly puzzled as to how I'd heard of them. I will tell you something; you and one other are the only persons I've known who could see them."

"Who could see them?" echoed Mr. Horrocks, astonished.

"Yes, I have made some experiments. You and I in that respect at least are privileged people."

"And that other?" asked Mr. Horrocks, after a pause.

"She is dead," replied Landen quietly.

Mr. Horrocks was silent for a while. Presently he said: "Was Ash very dark and did he limp slightly?"

"Yes," replied Landen.